HIGHLAND BLOOD

THE CELTIC BLOOD SERIES, BOOK 2

MELANIE KARSAK

CLOCKPUNK PRESS

**Trigger warning: Gentle reader, please be aware that this novel deals with
difficult topics surrounding violence toward women.*

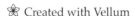 Created with Vellum

For the survivors

.

CHAPTER ONE

I took two hesitant steps into the darkness. Thora bumped against my leg. My head felt dizzy. My temples pounded. A sharp pain seared across my forehead, making me wince. It was all I could do to stay upright. Thora began to whimper when the darkness didn't pass. We were stuck between worlds. The silence was thick and heavy, the darkness tangible. If I didn't focus, we could get lost forever in the in-between space, neither the realm of the living nor the otherworld. I shuddered at the thought. I forced myself to concentrate past the pain racking my body. I could feel the living, breathing world just beyond my grasp. It was like someone had dropped a black veil between me and the realm of the corporeal. I breathed in deeply, trying to inhale the smell of earth, to hear the sounds of nature, to feel the living energy which belonged to the world of men.

It felt like an eternity before the sound of trickling water came to my ears. The sharp, tangy scent of mud filled my nostrils. We'd made it back. We were in the realm of the living but where? It was so dark. I took a few steps forward but my foot caught on something, and I fell into the wet mud face first. Thora whined. I reached out in the darkness and felt mud, roots, water, and gritty stone. We were in a cave. Water dripped from roots overhead. The air was spiced with elemental smells. I rose and wiped the mud off my face and out of my mouth. Carefully, I reached out and touched the cave wall. It was wet and slimy.

Using the cave wall as a guide, I worked my way forward. Water trickled over my hand, down my arm, and into my dress. My foot slipped. When I reached out to steady myself, I felt the soft body of a bat. It screeched and flew out of the cave.

I jarred sideways and fell into the mud again.

Thora whimpered.

"It's okay, girl. We'll get out of here, and everything will be okay," I said, trying to convince both her and myself.

It was too dark to see, but I knew my hands, knees, and elbows were bleeding. Mud worked into the cuts. The wounds stung. I dashed away hot tears of frustration and tried to keep my focus on my task. This was just a small inconvenience. My physical body could survive this discomfort. At the end of this trial, my love would be waiting for me. A marriage contract...finally, Madelaine had secured my match with Banquo.

"Let's go," I told Thora then pushed forward again.

Sliding and falling repeatedly, I walked in the darkness. My clothes were completely soaked and covered in sludge. I was bleeding. My hair was caked with muck and leaves. I must have looked like one of the fey things from the Hollow Hills. As the thought crossed my mind, I remembered the skeleton in Ynes Verleath...the Lord of the Hollow Hills. He was no legend. I had seen his skeleton. And if he had lived, what about those strange creatures that were rumored to roam the earth's belly? Were they real too? I suddenly felt eyes on me. It was as if I had summoned them with my very imagination. Were the little people of the Hollow Hills, vicious creatures of legends, watching me? If I failed to leave their realm, what would happen to me? I trembled.

Startling me from my terror, however, Thora barked and ran ahead.

I squinted. A dim light appeared at the end of the cave. I could hear the rain and the sound of the wind rushing through leaves.

"Thank you," I whispered and pushed ahead.

A moment later, I found myself standing at the mouth of a cave in the side of a mountain. It was raining heavily and must have been just hours before dark. Lightning shot across the sky, followed by the rolling sound of thunder. A screech owl shrieked somewhere in the distance. The cliffside was mud-washed. From the looks of things, it had been raining for days.

Thora paced back and forth, looking for a way down. Finally, she gave up and ran down the hillside. She looked up at me expectantly.

"Patience," I whispered. Stepping carefully onto the muddy hillside, I crouched down and slid down the side of the hill, grasping at roots and grass to keep from tumbling over. Something sharp dug into my palm, slicing open the hand I'd cut during my handfasting. At last, I reached the bottom. I was caked with grime from head to toe.

"When I see Andraste again, she's going to hear about this," I told Thora as I reached under my skirts to my petticoat. It was wet but relatively clean. I ripped off a piece of fabric and mopped up the blood pooling in my palm. Pain shot up my arm. I'd need to see Epona at once. A cut like that could get infected easily. I tried to catch some rainwater to wash my palm, but my hand was bleeding profusely. I poured the red liquid onto the leaves. It dripped down my arm. The image of my hands covered in so much blood made me swoon. I leaned against a tree and tied my hand up, hoping it would stop the flow.

Exhaling deeply, I looked around. I didn't recognize the forest.

"I'm too exhausted. My magic is spent. I don't know if I can get us back. Can you lead us?" I asked Thora.

She barked, set her nose to the ground, and moved forward. The forest was alive with noise. The wind blew. Rain patted on the leaves. Birds called. Ynes Verleath was a silent place. It jarred my senses to hear the cacophony. Thora moved with purpose, and we walked through the dark forest, following her instincts which, given my state, I trusted better than my own. It grew dark. The rain slowed to a steady patter. The air around us became thick with mist, making our travel even more difficult. Walking in the haze—with my spirit already worn so thin by time spent in Ynes Verleath—worried me. The veil between the worlds was always porous in the fog. One could walk in and out of time and space without even realizing it. And I felt like I was half between the worlds already. I forced myself to focus on the real world, on the realm of the living, and pushed myself forward, following Thora.

All my senses were on edge, so when a red deer blasted out of the brush, I yelped. Thora, who had not had the opportunity to chase game in so long, took off through the woods after it.

"Thora, come back here. Thora!"

She ran over a knoll and disappeared into the mists and darkness.

"Thora!"

There was no use. She wouldn't come back until

she'd given chase. I followed the direction toward which Thora was leading us. Soon, I came to a narrow cart path. I didn't know where I was, but at least I knew I was headed somewhere. I walked alone in the rain, trying to catch my bearings. Suddenly, I heard the sound of jangling metal and rough voices. Riders. I could see the light of torches coming down the path toward me. I had to get out of sight. Moving quickly, I dodged behind a thicket. Thorns scraped my skin as I struggled to hide, but I soon realized there wasn't enough cover. Moments later, the party came trotting down the road.

From the cover of brush, I could see there were seven men in the party. They wore heavy armor.

"Halt," one of them called then reined his horse forward. "Come out, girl."

I froze.

"No use in hiding. We saw you on the road. So unless you are a fey thing, come and stand before your betters."

I took a deep breath and reminded myself to stay calm. Covered in mud from head to toe, no one would ever recognize me. Perhaps they were but lost in the woods. I would play the role of a dumb woodland girl. Surely, they would not see Boite's daughter under the grime.

I stepped out of my hiding spot. When I got a better view, however, I was shocked to discover that not only were the men well-armored, but they were bearing my uncle's—King Malcolm's—standard. The men held their torches aloft. Their armor glimmered. I steeled my nerve. I was a poor woodsman's daughter. I was nothing. I was no one.

A young man in the group rode up to me. Pulling on his horse's reins, he rode in a circle around me. "What are you doing out so late, woman?" he asked.

My mind raced. If I revealed who I was, maybe these men could take me back to Madelaine. But then again, Boite had many enemies at court. His daughter might not be safe with the King's men. Better to just play the role I'd picked.

"Beggin' your pardon, your Lordship. I'm on my way back to my farm. Got delayed in the rain."

Even as I spoke the words, a tremor ran down my spine which told me that this excuse would serve me no better than revealing my true identity. In the end, I was a woman, alone, in the woods. The young man who looked down at me had eyes that shimmered the way Alister's once had. I could feel the predatory wolf inside him. His dangerous appetite effervesced from him stronger than the stench of his horse. My heart froze. Thora? Where was Thora?

"My Prince," an older man in the group called, "this is not the time—"

"Silence," the young man replied then pulled off his helmet.

"Yes, Prince Duncan," the man muttered then looked away.

I stepped backward. Prince. Prince? No. This was Duncan, son of Crinian and Bethoc, grandson of Malcolm. My cousin.

"Hold an arrow on her. She looks like she wants to run," Duncan said to his companion as he dismounted.

"It's raining, My Prince. The men are hungry and tired of riding. We've got a long night ahead of us. Must we—"

"All the more reason then," Duncan said. "Don't worry. I'll let the boys have a turn when I'm done. I'll get her loose and ready for the lads," he said with a laugh which the others joined. He then turned to me. "Now, where are you going, girl?" Duncan asked me as he strode forward.

Trembling, I stepped backward. I tried to calm myself, to call the raven, but all I could feel was the beating of my heart in my throat. Fear gripped me. I couldn't focus. I couldn't concentrate. All I could feel and hear was the pounding of my heart. *Run*, I told myself. *Run*. I eyed the man holding an arrow on me. He shook his head.

"My Lord, I beg you. Please don't," I whispered.

"Oh, come now, girl. Don't you want a royal bastard?"

I froze.

Morrigu? Scotia? Where are you? Help me!

A strange, hollow silence came in reply. I felt eyes on

me, like someone watched, their sorrow palpable, but no one came to my aid.

I closed my eyes and tried to call the raven once again, but was jerked from my thoughts when Duncan grabbed me roughly by the arms and pushed me face down on the ground near the thicket.

"Are you a virgin, girl?" he whispered as he pushed away my wet and muddy dress. I could feel drops of rain fall on my bare skin.

Holding me down with one hand, I heard him fussing with his buckles. "Dirty, filthy clothes. Don't you have anything better than this? Such a nice body hidden under such rags."

"No, no. Please. Don't," I whispered.

He struck the back of my head hard. Black dots and flashes like stars appeared before my eyes. Once again, pain shot through my head.

I cried out in agony.

"Shut up," he whispered. I felt his fingers between my legs, prodding. Moments later, he found what he was looking for. He grabbed my hips roughly and pulled me toward him, slamming his cock into me. My whole body shook as he invaded me.

"No," I whimpered as he beat himself into me. "No, no."

"Shut up," he said between breaths. He grabbed my hair and pulled it hard.

I closed my eyes and tried to trick myself. I told myself that it was Banquo. I told myself that I was with my love. I lied to myself. I tried to make myself believe this wasn't happening. I felt the rain on my naked skin, my flesh exposed for the world to see. I felt him inside me. Him. My cousin. Prince Duncan. Against all chance, I lay with my cheek pressed against the earth as my cousin assaulted me.

Banquo. My Banquo. Soon I would be with Banquo.

I don't know how long he took his pleasure, but some time later I heard Duncan groan then pull away.

"Nice," he said with a whisper. I could hear him buckling up his trousers. "Get up, girl." He kicked me over with his boot.

Out of my mind, I struggled to my feet, pushing my messy dress down. I stood across from him. This time, however, I stared him in the face.

His eyes were set close together and cloudy blue in color. His lips were fat, the bottom lip protruding noticeably. He had red blemishes all over his face. He looked nothing like my father. He must have taken after his father's line. Gold curls, damp from the rain, fell onto his shoulders. He stood fumbling inside his vest.

When he finally looked up at me, he seemed surprised to see me looking at him.

"Well," he said with a smile. "A pretty face after all. For your trouble." He tossed a bag of coins at my feet. With that, he turned around and mounted his horse once more.

"We gettin' a turn?" one of the men called.

"No," Duncan replied. "I feel better now. And it's still raining. Let's go. I'll get you a nice dry serving wench when we arrive."

"Two!" one of the men replied with a laugh.

"Even better," Duncan said, then spurred his horse away. As they rode off, I heard them fall into conversation about the luxuries of bedding two women at once.

The man holding the arrow on me lowered his weapon. "Don't come looking for any handouts for any bastards. We kill girls who try to ruin the prince's reputation. Understand me?"

I studied every inch of the man's face: dark hair, brown eyes, and a scar running across his forehead. He wore a badger sigil on his breastplate. I raised one finger and pulled what little bit of power I could muster from the air with my shaking hand then pointed it at his insignia.

I nodded. "No heirs," I more breathed than said, feeling my curse flow into the ether.

"MacDuff!" Duncan called back to the man.

MacDuff, as Duncan had named him, snarled at me then turned and rode back to his prince.

I bent and picked up the coin pouch. Burned onto the leather was the prince's emblem. The men's torchlight disappeared as they rode away. Their voices, their laughter, carried on the wind until I could hear them no more.

My stomach shook. A sick feeling racked me as I felt

his leavings drip down my leg. I turned and vomited. My body trembled. The woods grew dark again.

Some time later, Thora emerged from the darkness. When she caught the scent of the men, she growled.

"Run, Thora," I whispered. "Take us home."

Thora turned and raced through the woods. I moved quickly behind her, rushing through the wet grass, slogging through a stream, pushing through mud. There was a strange howling sound echoing through the woods. When I listened to it more closely, I realized it was my own sobbing I heard. I stopped, took a deep shuddering breath, then ran again.

Sometime later that night, I stumbled, out of my mind, into the coven. As soon as I realized where I was, I walked to the cauldron and collapsed.

CHAPTER TWO

"*C*erridwen?" Epona whispered softly. She lifted me gently, guiding me with soft hands toward her house.

I shuddered when she touched me.

"Cerridwen?"

I wanted to answer her, but I just couldn't.

Epona directed me inside then sat me down on a stool before the fire.

Wordlessly, she set an extra log on the fire while I stared absently into the glowing embers, my body trembling uncontrollably. I could hear Epona gathering jars from her cupboard. She appeared before me a few moments later.

"You're injured. May I tend to your wounds?" she asked carefully.

I nodded mutely. My mind was spinning around and

around. What had happened? Had that actually happened? My mind and body felt disconnected. I stared into the fire, stunned into disbelief.

"We need to get this dress off you. You'll take a chill. And it's...ruined."

She took my bag from me and set it aside. When she went to take the coin purse from my hand, however, I didn't let go. I held the proof in my hand, proof that the nightmare was real, proof that beyond all chance I had met my cousin in the woods, and he had violated me. If not for the coin pouch, I would not have believed my own mind.

Gently, Epona pulled my dress off then wrapped a heavy bear fur around me. Then she began washing me. First, she washed my face. I could see her eyes studying me, but I felt as if I had gone off to some strange place. An overwhelming sense of numbness shattered me. Epona's touch, which had always been warm and comforting, felt strange. I wanted to push her away, but I forced myself to be calm. In my heart, I knew I was with someone who loved and cared for me. I was safe. But still, I could barely abide it. I shut off my feelings and stared into the fire. My head felt woozy. Sweat trickled my forehead, and I felt myself swoon. A sharp pain shot through my head.

Strange images appeared before my eyes. I saw Banquo on a battlefield before a large army, rousing the assembly to war. And then I saw the raven-haired man from the cauldron. He was sitting on the throne of Scone. He smiled at me, but then his eyes turned to someone at my side. I looked down to see I was holding the hand of a small boy around six years old. He smiled up at me, his curly mop of dark hair sweetly framing his face, offsetting his pale blue eyes.

I gasped and rose.

"Cerridwen?"

"Bring me the blue flask," I said with urgency, grabbing Epona by the shoulders. "Now! Epona! Bring me the blue flask," I said, shaking her. When Gwendelofar had first revealed she was pregnant, Epona had offered her a concoction of herbs to rid herself of the child. The brew had been kept in a blue flask.

The vision. The strange sensation that had overcome me. I knew then, without a doubt, I was carrying Duncan's seed.

"Cerridwen," Epona said, looking me deep in the eyes. "Sit," she said, lowering me back onto my seat. She covered me with the fur once more. Epona then kneeled on the floor before me and closed her eyes. She was saying an incantation. I could just catch the words she recited. But more than that, I saw the glow that suddenly surrounded her. After a moment, she became silent, and the glow faded.

"Yes. You are with child." Once more, she took my hand. Gently, she took the coin pouch. It was stained with my blood. I heard her inhale sharply when she saw the insignia on the bag. "Duncan?"

"Yes," I whispered.

"He travels south after his meetings with the lords in the north," Epona said. "The blue flask…a child is but an innocent thing. Tidings that begin as foul can become fair. Wash the memory of what has happened from your mind. You are to be wed within the fortnight. Take your new husband to bed right away. No one will ever know."

"I can't betray Banquo like that," I replied. "I will tell him the truth."

"Banquo?"

"Sid said my marriage is confirmed."

"It is. To Gillacoemgain of Moray."

"Gillacoemgain of Moray!" My mind raced back in time to a conversation I'd once shared with Banquo who'd mentioned Gillacoemgain had taken power in Moray. Madelaine, as well, had once listed him as a man who might seek to take my hand.

Epona pushed my hair away from my face. "Malcolm has agreed to wed you to Moray. The matter is settled."

"But Epona, Banquo and I are soul-bound!"

"So Cerridwen and Banquo may be, but the law of the land has decreed the daughter of Boite shall marry the Mormaer of Moray."

I shook my head. "I will not."

"You must. You have no choice. Will you deny Moray

for Lochaber and start a war in the process? Will you condemn the man you love?"

"No, it's just…"

"A marriage by law."

"My marriage to Gillacoemgain is a betrayal of my ties to Banquo under the eyes of the old gods."

"And how do you intend to explain that to Gillacoemgain? To King Malcolm? They will put your druid's head on a spike."

She was right. I knew it. I just couldn't bear it. "Epona," I breathed, then looked down at the coin purse. "In the fire…I saw Duncan's child."

Epona looked into the flames then shook her head. "Perhaps you did. But the Great Mother has shown me more. I've seen two children."

"Children? Twins?"

Epona nodded then said, "They are your children, my girl. They are yours, not his."

"The blue flask—"

"No," Epona said. "You are stronger than that."

"I don't know if I can—"

"You can. You must. Gillacoemgain will never know. Let all the world rejoice when you have given heirs to Moray."

"But Epona," I cried, and this time I spoke the truth, "how can I love such children created by violence? Won't I despise them for how they took root in me? Will I look into their eyes and forever remember?" I shuddered.

"They are innocent. They are nothing more than flowers blooming in your womb. Will you weed them? They belong to no one but you."

"Epona, I don't know if I can..." I began to protest, but then I thought of the way the child in my vision had looked at me. He'd beamed up at me with pure love in his eyes.

"Promise me you will come here when the children are born. Promise me," Epona said.

"Of course," I replied, but I was so confused. What had happened? What was happening to me? First Duncan...now, Gillacoemgain of Moray? "Epona, where is Banquo?"

Epona shook her head. "I don't know. I haven't seen him for many months." Epona wore a strange expression on her face. Suddenly, I was very certain she wasn't telling me something.

"What is it?"

"Please forgive me. I..." Epona said then paused. "When Banquo came last, he demanded to know your whereabouts. He spoke of seeing you in the flames, in the dark places. I believe he left here under the impression you were lost to the otherworld, that you would not return."

"And you let him believe that?"

"I thought it best. I know how much you loved one another, but that fate is not meant to be. I wanted to make it easier for him. For you. I thought, perhaps, if he believed you were lost then he could move on. And, with him doing so, it would make it easier for you upon your return. There was never any hope for your marriage to Lochaber. I'm sorry, Cerridwen. I hoped to make the separation easier."

"How could you?" I whispered.

"My child, Gillacoemgain of Moray waits for you at Madelaine's keep. You must put Banquo from your mind. Please listen to my counsel in this. For Gillacoemgain. For you. For the seeds you carry. For Banquo. Cerridwen's time is done. Gruoch must return. You have duties. For the good of the realm, you must attend them. The Goddess needs you in this world now. She needs Gruoch."

Her words were an echo of Andraste's...Andraste who had warned of the wickedness that would cross my path. Had she known?

"And where was my goddess when I was face down in the mud?" I asked, looking once more at the coin purse. My body shook, and I tried to push the memories away.

"Still within you. Vengeance can be yours, but it is Gruoch, not Cerridwen, who will see to that."

I stared at the flames, and this time I saw my hands clutching a dagger, blood dripping from my fingers.

From deep within me, the raven called.

CHAPTER THREE

*M*adelaine embraced me the moment she entered Epona's house the following morning. Her crushing hug was nearly more than I could take. My body still felt so hollow. I felt like a ghost, a spirit moving through the tangible world. It was an odd feeling. I tried to shake the thought and focus on my beloved aunt. She looked older. The hair at her temples had turned gray. How much time had passed?

"I'm so glad you made it here so quickly. We thought it would take you much longer," she said.

"Yes, well, I was pushed out immediately," I replied. Pushed into darkness and damnation. Was I pushed fast so I would not miss my fate? Had Andraste known? When I saw her next, she would have a lot of explaining to do.

"A week's wait doesn't feel immediate to your impatient aunt."

"A week?"

Madelaine nodded.

Uald entered the house behind her. "So, she returns from the void."

I mustered up the best smile I could.

"Sit, sit," Madelaine said, motioning me toward the table. "You look pale, Corbie. Has she eaten, Epona?"

"Yes," Epona said distractedly as she rummaged about in her pantry.

I'd stayed the night with Epona in a kind of stupid slumber, half awake and half in the otherworld. It was so hard to collect myself. I felt like I was drunk, lost in the shadows, a fey and broken thing.

"How are you, my little love? You don't look like you feel well," Madelaine said.

"The walk between the worlds is grueling," Epona answered for me.

Madelaine smiled. "I've missed you so much." She took my hands. I winced when she touched the bandaged cut on my palm. "Oh, you're hurt?"

In so many ways. "I fell."

Madelaine nodded.

Uald, who'd taken a seat alongside me, was studying both me and Epona carefully. Madelaine was delighted to see me and that joy blinded her. Uald, however, gave me a questioning look.

I shook my head and looked away. Not now.

"Your betrothed waits for you at my castle. He has come with a full entourage to see you. You will be taken north to Moray where you will be wed. He is older than you, in his late thirties, I believe. He's tall and muscularly built. He has light brown hair and dark eyes. All in all, he is rather handsome."

I frowned. In all this puzzling madness, I had assumed that Gillacoemgain of Moray would be my raven-haired man. In the very least, that would have made sense. But he wasn't. And he wasn't Banquo. What in the world was I to do?

"Who cares what he looks like? All of Scotland knows he's a dangerous and bloody man," Uald said.

Madelaine frowned. "Yes, there was bloodshed. That is true," Madelaine said then turned to me. "Gillacoemgain killed his brother Findelach in civil war."

"Donalda's husband?" I asked then, remembering the story. Malcolm's younger daughter Donalda had been married to Findelach, the Lord of Moray. Findelach had fallen out of King Malcolm's favor and many whispered that the king supported Gillacoemgain's move to wrestle power from Findelach.

Madelaine nodded. "The same."

"Has Findelach no sons?" Uald asked.

"One, Macbeth, who sought protection from Lord Thorfinn of Orkney when his father was murdered."

"I'm sure that went over well," Uald said with a laugh. It was well known that Thorfinn of Orkney opposed Malcolm and wanted to rule the north of Scotland himself. With a powerful ally like Macbeth, who was an heir to Moray, the two would be a strong opposing force, one that Banquo had once told me he supported.

Madelaine nodded. "Indeed, until Macbeth was captured and handed over to his grandfather. He's now a ward in Malcolm's court."

"A prisoner, you mean," Uald said.

Madelaine shrugged. "Either way, he is subdued. Your marriage to Gillacoemgain will give you rule over the ancient kingdoms. It is a great honor."

"Easy for you to say. No one seems to care that I am already bound to the heir of Lochaber," I said angrily. My own rage startled me. My heart pounded in my chest.

Madelaine shifted in her seat. "I swear by the Great Mother, I did try."

"We thought we heard a raven's caw," Sid said then, pushing the door open. When she entered, she immediately sensed the tension in the room. "Ah, so I see you've told her the good news."

In spite of myself, I chuckled.

Sid flopped down into the seat beside me and put her arm around me. "Gillacoemgain of Moray, the fratricide. Excellent choice, Madelaine," she told my aunt then turned to me. "Well, Raven Beak, there's always the next life for love."

Madelaine opened her mouth to protest but then closed it, thinking better of it.

"Cerridwen?" another voice called from the door. I turned to see Aridmis there.

"Sister."

"Many welcome returns," she said, smiling at me. "The stars told me you were coming soon."

"Do they have anything else to say?" I asked sourly.

"Much, actually," Aridmis said knowingly.

"I'm weary of the future," I said, suddenly feeling very tired.

Aridmis poured a glass a water and lifted it, "then let's toast the past."

I smiled wryly at her, lifting my cup.

She smiled sympathetically at me, nodding in assent.

Druanne and Bride then entered. They'd been discussing something heatedly.

"You don't always have to be right," Bride was telling Druanne.

"I'm not saying—" Druanne began but Bride cut her off when she saw me.

"Merry met! It's Cerridwen!"

Druanne looked sharply at me, plastering on a false smile. She nodded to me then busied herself helping Epona.

"You don't look a day older," Bride told me.

"Yet feel the weight of a thousand years on me," I said absently.

Bride laughed, "Pshaw, so complain the young when they don't know better. Just wait until you're so old that you don't recognize yourself in the looking glass anymore."

The company in the room fell into cheery laughter. The conversation regarding Gillacoemgain of Moray was put on hold, and with Druanne there, I did my best to put my troubles out of mind. The last thing I wanted was for her to know what had happened. I was still coming to grips with it myself and didn't want her poking at my wounds. But with the others came noise. And while having those I loved near me made me feel comforted, the loud sounds started clanging on my nerves.

"I know someone else who has missed you," Uald said. "Why don't we go check on Kelpie?"

Grateful for her intervention, I followed Uald outside. The bright sunlight hurt my eyes.

"I've had some luck breeding. We managed one colt, but no more. I need to bring in a fresh mare. Unfortunately, I'll be losing my stallion now."

"I'll have horses sent to you. Madelaine can bring them when she comes next."

Uald laughed. "Spending the wealth of Moray already?"

"What else will I have to do in Moray, wed to a man I do not love?"

Uald leaned against the fence. "Banquo...he came, you know, searching for you. Epona led him to believe you would not return."

"So she confessed."

"Epona doesn't know that I told him you would return. But I did warn him that marriage was out of the question."

"Uald," I whispered. "Where is he?"

"North, with Lord Thorfinn. At the moment, he is allied with your promised husband's enemies."

"What should I do?"

"Well, if you ask me, I say you should run off and tell Malcolm to go to hell. You and your druid don't need the court life."

"You tempt my heart."

Uald whistled, capturing Kelpie's attention. My horse sniffed the wind then trotted over to me. Kelpie stuffed his nostrils in my hair and breathed deeply.

"I missed you too," I whispered, stroking his neck. I turned back to Uald. "I don't know what to do."

"It's your choice. If you return to court, return as Boite's daughter and wield your bloodline like a weapon. But never let Cerridwen sink below your skin. Be a raven amongst doves."

It was then I noticed a young horse moving across the field toward us. "Who is that?" I asked.

"The offspring I told you about. I named him Titan."

"He's enormous."

The horse stopped in front of Uald who scratched his ears. "He's no bigger than he should be." Uald looked at me and then frowned. "It is the same with Sid. Corbie, you've been gone a long time."

"Long? How long?"

"Six years."

"Six years!" Six years was too much. No one could wait that long. Banquo would have given up on me already. I closed my eyes and shook my head. As I did so, I felt a sharp pain shoot across my skull. I stepped away from the fence. My knees grew soft.

"Cerridwen," Uald said, catching me before I fell.

"It's too much," I whispered.

"Come," Uald said, leading me to her smithy. "I made something for you."

Once inside, I sat down at the table and held my head in my hands while Uald dug through her trunk. A few moments later, she set a package in front of me.

"Go ahead," she told me.

Trying to ignore the pain, I slowly unwrapped the bundle. Inside, I found a glimmering sword topped with a raven's head. It was the most beautiful weapon I'd ever seen.

I gasped. "Did you make this?"

"In many ways, you are the daughter I never had. Take this sword, and wield it as the raven."

I rose and lifted the blade. My sword arms were weaker than they had been before I'd gone to Ynes Verleath, but I was still strong. Bracing myself, I swished the blade back and forth. Before my eyes, I imagined Duncan's monstrous face. I envisioned taking his head off. But it didn't feel like enough. It didn't feel violent enough. I wanted more blood. I heard my heart beating hard, and in the distance, I perceived the sound of raven's wings.

"Uald, daughter of Hephaestus," Madelaine called from behind me. "Isn't it beautiful? Don't you just love it?"

I turned and looked at Madelaine.

The expression on Madelaine's face changed. She looked startled. "Corbie?"

"It is the raven you see," Uald told her. "Don't be afraid."

I lowered the sword, and the sound of wings dissipated. My heartbeat slowed.

"It's beautiful," I told Uald.

"I...I was thinking we should get ready to go. Tavis is waiting. It's been a week. I don't want to keep Moray waiting longer. They...they think I've traveled to the convent for you," Madelaine said, obviously upset. I wondered then how I looked when the raven took over me.

I lifted the belted scabbard off the table and wrapped

it around my waist. Sliding the sword inside, I crossed the smithy and embraced Uald.

"Thank you," I whispered in her ear. "For everything."

"If you need anything, we are always here for you."

I nodded then turned to Madelaine.

"I'll need to say goodbye to Sid," I told her.

Madelaine nodded. "She went back to her house. I'll let Epona know we are planning to leave."

"I'll get Kelpie ready. I'm sure he'll be keen to ride."

"Thank you, Uald," I said, setting my hand on her shoulder.

I turned then and crossed the square to Sid's little house. I knocked lightly on the door.

"Come," she called. She was already packing up my old things. "We stored your belongings here," Sid said. "I looked after them."

I nodded then sat down on Sid's bed. I gently touched the hem of one of my old dresses. So much life had passed. Six years. How had that happened? I sighed heavily.

"That sigh says a lot of things," Sid commented. "I'd sigh too if I had to get married."

"And to the wrong man, nonetheless."

"You are lucky to have so many to choose from."

"Am I? Soon I'll be in Moray counting bricks on the wall."

"You will be in charge of the women. You can force them to like you."

"Am I so awful that I need to force people to like me?"

"Yes, but at least you will have the power to do so."

I smiled. "Be careful or I may just force you to come with me."

"If only I could. The wrong man, eh?"

"Wrong man. Wrong title. Wrong lands. Wrong, wrong, wrong. So much is wrong here, Sid."

"One man is as good as another."

"You don't really believe that."

"The only difference from one man to the other is the color of his hair."

"You have a poor opinion of men."

Sid stilled then turned and looked at me. "Shouldn't you?"

I stared at her. Did she know?

"Nadia," Sid said gently. "The fey saw."

I felt like someone had wrapped their hands around my throat. Terrible shame swept over me, but then that shame turned to anger. Why should I feel disgraced because of the evil in others? "The fey should not gossip other's sorrows."

"It was not gossip. They were afraid for you. They have foreseen…life springing forth in you."

"Yes."

"What are you going to do?"

"Take my new husband to bed as soon as I can force myself to do so, give the innocent flowers growing inside me a respectable family name, then avenge myself when the time comes."

"I have taken that offense more times than I care to say."

"He will pay."

"May the Morrigu let it be so," Sid said then smiled at me. "You will be a mother."

I nodded as I studied my friend. I remembered what Epona had told me when I first came to the coven, that Sid had a child that lived amongst the fey...or so Epona believed. And worse still, I remember what Epona had said about the child Sid had killed in her madness after being sexually violated. "Sid..." I began, but I didn't know what to say.

She exhaled deeply then shook her head. "You are stronger than I am. You will be fine."

"What of your child?" I asked her. "Does your second child live?"

She nodded. "My sweet boy. He's nearly ten now and more fey than human," she said then shrugged. "Even in the unexpected, we can find blessings." She handed me my bag. I heaved it over my shoulder, and we turned and went outside.

Thora ran across the square and joined me.

Madelaine, Epona, and Uald were waiting with the horses, which were already saddled.

Aridmis crossed the coven square and took my hand. "All seems dark now," she told me, "but the clouds will pass. I've seen it in the stars."

"Thank you, dear sister," I told her.

Bride, too, waited for me. She handed me a bundle. "Honey cakes. It is a long ride to Moray."

I kissed her on both cheeks. "Thank you, Mother."

"I hope I will see you again in this life. If not, I'll find you in the next," Bride told me.

I inclined my head to her.

Druanne, who looked like she was smothering her jealousy, nodded to me. "Farewell, Gruoch."

"Druanne," I replied stiffly then turned from her to look once more at Sid.

"Don't leave me alone. Please come and see me," I told her.

Sid nodded. "I will. Don't worry. We'll be together again. All of us." She pulled me into an embrace.

I felt tears threaten, but I choked them back.

I let her go then and went to Kelpie.

Uald helped me mount my horse. "Farewell," she told me. "May she ever keep you safe," she added, patting the scabbard.

"Thank you, Uald."

She nodded.

Once I was mounted, Epona came to me. "Remember your promise?"

"I remember."

"Fair travels," she said then let me go. "May the Mother Goddess watch over you."

"And you."

I smiled at Sid once more then tapped on the reins. Kelpie turned and we followed Madelaine out of the coven. I was leaving to wed, not Banquo, not my raven-haired man, but a complete stranger.

$\mathcal{I}$t had been awhile since I'd been on horseback, in Madelaine's company, or amongst normal, common people. I wondered how the world had changed. From what I'd seen so far, it was much the same. Men were as violent as ever, and my country was ruled by cutthroats. I stared at Madelaine's back as we rode into the forest. My mind felt like it was breaking apart at the seams. More than anything, all I wanted to do was run off and find Banquo. But six years was a long time. Surely he would have given up on me by now. Once more, I was the daughter of Boite, niece of the king of Scotland, and he'd commanded my marriage to Gillacoemgain of Moray. The raven in me wanted to defy them all. The spirit of Boudicca decried the outrage. And I nursed an awkward ache between my thighs and wondered about the children growing inside me. None of this felt real or true. In less than ten moons, I would be a mother. I had been a poor girl violated in the rain, and as a result, I would now raise my cousin's children. Where was the justice in that? And even worse, I questioned myself: was there any difference between being assaulted and whoring myself to Gillacoemgain of Moray? I wasn't sure. Nothing made sense.

Madelaine chatted as we rode through the woods. She told me about the entourage waiting for me. She also spoke of her new husband who, she said, praised her constantly. I could barely focus on her words. I set my hand on my stomach and tried to feel the life inside me. I felt different but no more than that strange sense of change. I knew I was pregnant. I'd seen the child in my vision. But Epona, whose prophecies were never wrong, had said I would bear twins. If so, why had I only seen one child?

"Madelaine?" I heard Tavis' familiar voice call.

"We're here," Madelaine told me.

So soon? Lost in my thoughts, I'd barely noticed the passage of time. Perhaps my body was not yet in tune with the world of the living after all.

"Gruoch," Tavis called, smiling with welcome. "More beautiful than ever."

"Merry met," I told him.

He saddled his horse quickly, and we all set off once more.

Memories flooded my mind as we rode back to the

castle. It seemed like yesterday that we'd traveled this path together. I was too naive then. I knew nothing of the world that lay beyond the castle walls. Now, I had felt a dark goddess' hand on my throat, traveled to the other world, and *I* was one of the Wyrd Sisters. Me. More than that, I was a killer. But I didn't regret what I had done to Alister. I was relieved to know I would never have to lay eyes on him again.

As we rode over the knoll toward the castle, a strange sensation overcame me. The person who'd lived behind those walls was dead now. The innocent girl who'd worried about her embroidery was lost. The castle looked smaller, and grimier, than I remembered. It paled in comparison with Ynes Verleath's decayed beauty.

The field outside the castle was full of tents that flew the banners of Moray. Farmers and tradesmen selling their wares intermingled amongst the strangers. The familiar stench of roasting meat and ale filled the air. I choked the anxiety that rose up in me as I thought of the ale hall and the men. Alister, I reminded myself, was gone. And I was no longer a girl who would sit idly by and watch. I hoped Gillacoemgain of Moray was prepared to wed a woman who would speak her mind. And if not, it mattered little to me, I would speak anyway.

Tavis led us through the front gate. I dismounted from Kelpie.

"I'll see to it that he has his old stall. No doubt he'll be anxious to meet the new herd," Tavis told me, taking charge of my steed.

I patted Kelpie on the neck then handed my bags to the fleet of servants who'd met Madelaine and me at the door.

"So where is my fiancé?" I asked.

"Most likely in conference with my husband. They will give you a chance to freshen up before you make his acquaintance," Madelaine replied.

I rolled my eyes. Wonderful. Just what I needed, a man who expected me to look like a pampered pet.

Madelaine then led me to a room on the opposite end of the castle from where both she and I used to stay. "We'll leave old memories on the other end of the castle," Madelaine said, opening the door to one of the large guest chambers. The room was airy and nicely decorated. Bright tapestries covered the walls. A fire was burning, and a wash tub had already been set out.

"I took the liberty of having a few dresses made for you."

"Thank you," I said absently as I eyed the place. "It's all so lovely."

"Gruoch…I am sure you feel very strange being here. I know you are unhappy. When I was wed to Alister—"

"Please. No. Think nothing of it. It is only the strangeness I feel after my time in the otherworld."

"Epona said you were with the Wyrds," Madelaine said, her forehead furrowing. "Such a dark place. Such dark magic," she whispered. "That look on your face in Uald's smithy. It reminded me of something that happened the night Alister had died. I heard…I heard a raven."

I shook my head as if to say I didn't want to speak of it.

Understanding, Madelaine nodded.

A moment later there was a knock on the door.

"My Lady? We're here to assist Lady Gruoch if she's ready?"

Madelaine raised an eyebrow at me.

I nodded.

"Come," Madelaine called. "I'll go now and make myself suitable. Someone will come from the hall to fetch you."

I nodded again.

"So pleased to have you home," she whispered once more, kissing my cheeks. "Even if just for a couple of days!"

I smiled. Madelaine was as bright and cheery as ever. It was hard to feel sullen around her.

She left me then with a fleet of serving women who set about heating my bathwater. They perfumed the bath with something that smelled of roses. The hot water sent spirals of steam up in the cool air.

When they moved to take my clothes off, however, I stopped them.

"No, I'll see to it myself."

"Are you sure, My Lady? We always help your aunt."

"Yes. I'm certain."

With that, the women left me.

I pulled off my gown, dropping the sweaty garment on the floor, and lowered myself into the warm tub. The ladies had left all manners of combs, creams, and oils beside the wash basin. I took my time, feeling the water.

"Wash away the terror," I said, dripping water over my skin. "Let my heart be light again. Let my heart be free again."

Once I was clean, I rose and rubbed my limbs with the perfumed oils. I then sat down before the looking glass and brushed out my long, dark hair, braiding it from the temples. I affixed it with a silver comb sitting on my dresser. I then slipped on a purple gown I found in my wardrobe. When Madelaine said she'd had a few dresses prepared, she wasn't joking. The wardrobe was full. The purple dress was much the same color as the clothes I'd worn in Ynes Verleath. When I was finally done, I studied myself in the looking glass. I had been transformed. Cerridwen was gone. Once more, I was the daughter of Boite. And when I looked at my reflection, I saw my father in my features: dark hair, heather-colored eyes. I closed my eyes and took a deep breath, calling up the deep well of energy inside me. I just brushed its surface, and from it, I took strength. Opening my bag, I took out the raven amulet and torcs I'd found in Ynes Verleath and put them on. I turned then, not waiting for any royal summons, and headed downstairs to meet the man who would usurp Banquo's love and title.

CHAPTER FIVE

I traveled down the familiar hallways to the first floor of the castle. Once more, the ale hall was brimming with rowdy laughter and loud talk. But something was different. The scene inside was nothing like the drunken Sodom and Gomora that Alister had preferred. Instead, I found nicely dressed gentleman and ladies seated at the table. The fire burned cheerfully. Bread and wine heaped the table, but the meat had not yet been served. Had they been waiting for me? As well, the men who'd become such a familiar part of Alister's household were missing. Instead, I was greeted by the eyes of strangers. From their dress, I understood that these were the men of Fife, Madelaine's new husband, and of Moray, my fiancé. The room fell silent when I walked into the hall.

"Gruoch?" Tavis called. He'd been standing beside

the fireplace smoking a pipe and looking noticeably relaxed. It seemed that having Alister gone had brought relief to many.

Tavis crossed the room quickly and took my arm. "They didn't announce you."

"I know. I wanted to catch them off guard. Which is he?"

"Standing. End of the table," he said but turned me in a different direction. "My Lord of Fife," Tavis called, escorting me across the hall to a white-haired gentleman with a kind smile, short beard, and twinkling blue eyes. The man's stomach ballooned over his belt. "May I introduce the Lady Gruoch?"

I kept my gaze on the Thane of Fife but flicked my eyes just once to the tall man standing at the end of the table. He was watching me intently but said nothing. Madelaine was right. He was handsome. In the least, there was that. But he was not Banquo.

"My Lady!" the Thane said in surprise, reaching out to take my hand. "We would have sent a page for you. We thought to give you more time after your long journey."

"I've little use for waiting around," I replied.

The Thane looked taken aback by my words, but then he grinned. "So, you are like your aunt after all. I warned Moray that the line of MacAlpin didn't breed wilting flowers."

"Gruoch?" I heard Madelaine call from behind me.

She crossed the room to meet me. "How wonderful. I was just about to send someone to fetch you," Madelaine said, taking me from Tavis who stepped dutifully away.

"It is a pleasure to make your acquaintance, my uncle," I told the Thane. "The serenity of my aunt's smile has led me to be predisposed toward you already."

Madelaine's new husband smiled. "Well, I hope I can put a smile on your lovely face as well."

By the old gods, I hated courtly pleasantries. "I'm certain there is another gentleman in attendance that will vie for that right?" I said then cast a glance around.

The assembled audience giggled.

I scanned the room until my eyes fell on Moray. He stepped away from the end of the table and moved toward me. He was older than me, perhaps thirty-five years of age, but by no means old. He had squinting eyes and a rugged, square jaw. His tanned face spoke of days in the sun. He was clean-shaven and dressed in a handsome dark green tunic, the blue and green cloth of Moray, and recently-shined riding boots. Had he dressed up in anticipation of meeting me?

"It is my hope to best you, Fife, for the smile on this Lady's face," he said.

Remembering my manners, I curtsied to him.

"I am Gillacoemgain of Moray, Lady."

"I am glad that you are, or I would have offended my betrothed by falling in love with your countenance," I replied. *Play the game. I had to play the game.*

Gillacoemgain laughed quietly, his stance relaxing. "Well, I'm glad it pleases you. I see you take after your lovely aunt."

Gillacoemgain was playing the game too. I smiled. He was charming. I could deal with a charming man.

I inclined my head to him.

Fife clapped his hands happily. "Well done. Well done. Now that our fair ladies are here, let's have music and wine. What do you say, Moray?"

Gillacoemgain nodded.

A servant came forward and led Gillacoemgain and me to seats at the head of the table.

The hall erupted with the sound of flutes and lyres. The music was soft and sweet. Fife must have brought his own musicians with him. The servants from the kitchen, most of whom I recognized, began moving quickly about carrying large trays of food.

"How was your journey from the nunnery?" Gillacoemgain asked me then. He lifted the wine carafe and poured me a glass.

"Without consequence," I replied.

He smiled then, causing a dimple to form on his left cheek. He chuckled to himself.

"Something amusing?" I asked, sitting back into my chair.

Gillacoemgain shook his head. "No. It's only…I was told you've lived at the nunnery for several years. I expected a churchish girl. I was worried that you wouldn't fare well in Moray where the weather can be harsh. I see now my fears were unfounded. You take after your uncle."

"I'll assume you mean that as a compliment," I said, lifting my glass of wine.

Gillacoemgain laughed. "Oh, well, now I see the family resemblance even more clearly." He clinked his glass of wine against mine.

When Gillacoemgain drank, I set down my cup and waved to a servant I recognized.

"Aggie, isn't it?" I asked the girl.

"Yes, My Lady, and many welcomes home."

"Thank you, my dear. My dog, Thora, can you inquire where she is? If she's at the stables, tell them I want her brought here."

The girl nodded. "Yes, My Lady."

"Is something amiss?" Gillacoemgain asked.

I shook my head. "I'm certain you will find this as odd, but I have a dog that I dearly love and haven't seen since my arrival. I was concerned for her welfare."

"What manner of dog?"

"I don't know." I was pretty certain *a dog who can speak when you meet her in the otherworld* was not the answer he was looking for. "She is large and black."

"Mastiff, perhaps? Deerhound? Trained to hunt?"

"I've trained her to track."

"*You've* trained her to track?"

I nodded.

Gillacoemgain raised an eyebrow at me. "Is that a normal part of daily devotions at your nunnery?"

"Of course. Isn't it everywhere?"

Gillacoemgain eyed me closely. "You are an interesting woman, Gruoch."

"And what about you? Are you an interesting man, Gillacoemgain of Moray?"

"Depends on what you're interested in."

"Well," I said with a sidelong smile, "I guess we'll have to learn what we have in common."

"I look forward to that."

It was not long after that Thora was brought discreetly into the hall.

"Now that I have you in my sight, you must behave. Sit quietly here and stay out of trouble," I told her.

Thora wagged her tail then went under the table and put her head on my feet.

"She acts as though she understands you," Gillacoemgain said.

"We've been together a long time. We understand one another."

He nodded appreciatively. "I, too, am fond of animals. Dogs, horses, but especially birds...but I've never trained a dog to track. Will you teach me?"

"I'll do anything you wish, My Lord."

"Then sons for Moray, Lady. Straight off."

"Of that, I can assure you." *More than he could ever know.*

Gillacoemgain smiled.

Later that evening, after everyone had eaten and all the lords and ladies in attendance had introduced themselves to me, people began dancing. Gillacoemgain and I joined them.

He was very tall, and his arms were massive. I studied his body closely, trying to shut out all the images of Duncan. I tried to remember how nice it had felt to be with Banquo. I tried to remember the pleasure of being with a man. But it was hard to force myself to forget. If I wanted to survive this with my mind intact, I had to believe I wanted Gillacoemgain. I had to fool myself. I touched his body gently, feeling his strong arms. Being so close to him, our bodies pressed together, I caught his scent. He smelled of cedar and lavender.

"When will we be leaving for Moray, My Lord?" I asked.

He smiled then gently stroked the backs of my arms. I had to bury the instinct that made me want to pull away. I had to get past it. I had to.

"Tomorrow. But I'm afraid I will have to leave Moray shortly after we arrive."

"That's unfortunate. May I ask the reason?"

"There is discontent in the north. Our marriage should persuade Thorfinn to quiet his claim, but arms is often a better reminder than marriage vows. And sons, Gruoch, will further silence that half-Viking who would control my lands," he said, and this time I heard the angry edge under his voice.

"Well, we will have to get to work on those sons very soon," I replied playfully, letting my fingers dance along his neck.

He pulled me close. "Has the nunnery made you eager?" he asked.

"I wasn't eager until I looked upon you," I whispered in reply.

Blood. I would need to get some blood. I would need to stain the sheets to assure them that Gillacoemgain was my first, that I had given my maidenhead to my lawful husband.

Gillacoemgain pulled me closer, and this time I felt him. His cock was hard. He wanted me. I closed my eyes and inhaled deeply. When I felt and smelled him, feeling his protective arms around me, I questioned myself. Could I lust after such an act of violence? Did I have it in me to choose this man? Not just take him, but choose him? And in the end, when I took Gillacoemgain to bed, was I betraying the man I truly loved? *Banquo, where are you?*

CHAPTER SIX

That night, after the castle had quieted, I knelt before the fire in my chamber, Thora lying beside me. The embers popped and snapped. I knew what I needed to do, where I needed to go, but I just couldn't force my feet to make the walk between Gillacoemgain's bedchamber and my own.

I threw some herbs into a cauldron hanging over the fire. The sharp scents of sage and other herbs filled the room. I inhaled deeply and gazed into the flames. I felt hot but tried to ignore the trickles of sweat on my brow and running down my back. Focusing on the embers, I lulled myself into a trance. Loosening my spirit from the body, I forced myself to see the eternal flame of the Goddess in Ynes Verleath. A moment later, I found myself in the otherworld. The scent of wisteria overwhelmed me.

I walked, my form little more than a shadow, to the terrace where Andraste sat, leaning against her staff, by the fire.

"Cerridwen," she said without looking up at me.

"Did you know?"

"Know what?"

"Don't be coy. Did you know I would encounter Duncan? Did you know I was sent to marry Moray? Did you know what was going to happen?"

"Does it matter?" she replied then turned to face me. "In the end, does it matter? We are all fated to live the lives the gods have decreed for us. You will bear Duncan's children. And you will wed Moray."

"But what about Banquo?" I whispered.

"He's married another and fathered a child with her besides. Forget him."

"What!" I felt my physical body tremble. The sensation started to pull me back to the realm of the living.

"I speak the truth," Andraste said.

"You…you promised me a different title. Queen. I don't understand what's happening."

"You don't wish to be the Queen of the North? Aren't you satisfied to be the Queen of the Picts? Do you wish bigger feats than that of the sons of Alpin?"

"No."

"You carry the children of a prince. Would you rather their father to be your husband?"

I gasped. It was a possibility I had not thought of. "No."

Andraste turned back to the fire. "Be settled in Moray. The goddess will see to you."

"Is he really...has he really wed another?"

Andraste sighed deeply. "Yes. Forget your druid. Like you, he had to obey his father's will. And Epona let him think you were gone forever. What else could he do?"

Wait. He could have waited for me. "Nothing," I whispered.

Andraste nodded.

I let go.

I found myself lying in front of the fire in my bedchamber once more. The coals had burned low.

Thora licked my chin to rouse me.

Banquo. How could he? Had Epona's words truly left him in such despair? Had he believed me to be dead or beyond his reach, lost to the darkness? Tears streamed down my cheeks. I pitied him. I pitied the man I loved. He would have mourned me. He would have mourned the life he'd been dreaming of, as I did. I could go to him now, but at what cost? He was married. He had a woman and a child. He'd been wed out of political alliance. And if I left, what danger would I bring to my own house? I wiped the hot tears from my cheeks then shuddered. Pulling my knees to my chest, I rocked myself slowly back and forth. It was more than I could bear.

Banquo was lost to me. I'd been sexually assaulted. I was pregnant. I was about to be married off to a stranger and rejoin court life. My hands shook as I swayed slowly back and forth. I felt a strange pain shoot across my head. I closed my eyes and tried to breathe deeply, tried not to think about it all. Everything threatened to overwhelm me. It wanted to crash over me like a wave. If I let it, I might not survive it. I rocked and rocked. There was a way out of this. There was a way out of all this madness. I knew the herbs. I could end it myself. I could end…myself. It would be so easy.

An image flickered through my mind of the dark-haired child and his glimmering blue eyes.

Stop, I told myself. *Stop.*

My body stilled.

My hands stopped shaking.

I rose and stood before the flames. Maybe I would marry Moray as Gruoch, but Gruoch…she could not handle what had to be done next.

I pulled a dagger from my boot and stabbed my already-injured palm, cutting my handfasting scar in half. Reaching my arm over the dying flame, I poured the blood onto the hot coals. The liquid sizzled and filled the air with a strange smell. I closed my eyes and called the raven.

Come.

Come.

Come and we shall devour him together.

I heard raven wings beating, coming from afar. My

body shuddered when I felt the raven enter me, the dark spirit that was both me and not me, that was Cerridwen in her truest form, take control. I gazed around the chamber with my raven's eyes. I grabbed a brush and combed my long, dark hair, letting it fall loose over me. I then grabbed the small vial of chicken's blood I had gathered earlier that evening, slipping it into my robe pocket.

"Stay here," I told Thora, but it was the raven who spoke.

Thora tilted her head, studying me carefully, then lay down beside the fire.

Letting the raven have her way, I detached from my mind and watched as I exited my chamber and headed down the hallway to meet with Gillacoemgain of Moray.

*O*utside Gillacoemgain's door, one of the men from Gillacoemgain's company dozed in a chair. The raven eyed him curiously and determined he wasn't a threat. In fact, it was good if gossip spread about my midnight visit. As I drew near, the man woke.

"My Lady?" he asked.

"Is your Lord within?"

The man smiled knowingly. "Yes, My Lady."

"And he has no company?" For all I knew, Gillacoemgain could have ten whores in his room.

"No, My Lady. The Mormaer isn't that kind of man."

This answer pleased the raven. "Let me in."

"Of course, Lady Gruoch," he said then opened the door.

When the light shone in from the hall, Gillacoemgain stirred and rolled over.

"I need nothing, Fergus," he mumbled.

I walked quietly to the side of his bed and removed my robe. I then slipped into the bed with him.

Gillacoemgain woke instantly. "Gruoch?"

I moved my hands across his body and began to tug at his shirt while my mouth covered his, drowning any protests he may have made. He fell into my passionate kisses. The raven enjoyed his smell, the feel of his strong body, his taste, and his beauty. Gruoch, the part of me that still watched, saw the raven work with detachment.

When I finally gave his mouth a break, he said, "I was tempted to find your room this evening, but I thought I dare not be so bold. Yet here you are."

"I lay abed with my body burning for you. We are to be married. There is no reason to wait until Moray where you may only have a few chances to come to me before you must go. I hope you don't think me too forward. I don't act so with men. It is only knowing you will be my husband that allows me to act as my body wishes."

"No, no, your logic falls true. I had wished to say the same to you."

His hands found my breasts and touched them

gently. I kissed his neck and chest, and my hands roved over his strong back.

I am deceiving him.

We are deceiving him.

We are right.

It must be done.

His touch was different from Banquo's. Banquo had touched me tenderly, worshiping me. Banquo and I had shared the deepest core of ourselves. Soul magic. Gillacoemgain, on the other hand, played with my breasts, sucked my nipples, squeezed my ass, and stroked my hair. He enjoyed my body in the most physical of ways, and the raven returned the favor in kind. My mouth moved down his neck and across his shoulders. He was a powerful and skilled lover, as a man of his age would be. I was surprised when my body reacted with pleasure to his intimate caresses. And when he finally slipped inside me, the raven trembled with pleasure. Our bodies moved in tandem, and soon, we both found release. After, Gillacoemgain lay beside me, his head on my shoulder.

"Lovely woman," he whispered in my ear. "I never thought I'd have such a beautiful wife. I will cherish you always."

His soft and loving words quieted the raven. The dark wings retreated, and I felt myself, once more just Gruoch, lying in bed with the man who would be my husband.

"Are you thirsty? Would you like some wine?" he asked.

I shook my head. "Water?"

Gillacoemgain gently stroked my hair away from my face then rose and crossed the room to fetch his water pouch. I watched him as he walked. In truth, I was lucky. He was young and handsome. His body was sculpted from his days in battle, and his naked form was a sight to behold. Andraste was right. Malcolm could have married me to Duncan. Had he tried to do so I would have ended my own life. No one could suffer such a terrible fate.

"Here you are," Gillacoemgain said, handing me the skin. He sat beside me on the bed sipping a glass of wine. "Are you all right? Are you…are you in pain?" he asked carefully.

"Sore," I said, and it was the truth but not for the reasons he expected. "But I'll be fine."

Gillacoemgain smiled. "Gruoch, daughter of Boite. You look like your father. I saw him once when I was a teenager. I admired him greatly."

My heart was moved by his words. "I loved him dearly."

"Stay with me tonight? I…I don't want you to go."

I nodded.

Gillacoemgain smiled, kissed me on the forehead, then rolled into bed beside me. I took the last sip of water then set the skin aside. Gillacoemgain pulled me down beside him, wrapping his arms around me.

"Never in my wildest dreams did I think I would have a wife with a Pictish spark. I'm so pleased with you, Gruoch."

"M'Lord," I replied playfully.

Gillacoemgain laughed. "My bride," he whispered into my hair, then moments later he fell asleep.

I waited until he was completely lost to the world of dreams then reached for my robe. Grabbing the small vial from my pocket, I poured enough blood on the bedding to convince the household I'd kept up my end of the bargain. I then went to the window and looked outside. The moon was a sliver of silver on the starry canvas. *Banquo. Banquo, why did you give up on me?*

Sighing, I tossed the vial out the window and crawled back into bed with Gillacoemgain of Moray, the man who would soon be my husband and father to the children I carried.

CHAPTER SEVEN

I woke the next morning to the sound of servants. The women who'd attended me the previous day were stoking the fire and readying my clothes.

Disoriented, I sat up and looked around.

"Gillacoemgain?"

"He went to meet with the Thane of Fife," one of the serving maids told me. "His man, Fergus, sent us here to look after you."

"Ah," I said. "I must have walked here in my sleep."

"Common problem," the eldest of them replied with a laugh as she shook out my chemise. "Happens to many a young lad and lass. Come now, Lady. Let's get you dressed."

With the women's help, I dressed in a bright blue

gown then headed downstairs to look for Thora. She was waiting for me at the bottom of the main stairwell.

"I see the maids let you out. Find anything to eat?"

She wagged her tail happily. Since she wasn't dancing in circles and jumping all over me, I assumed that meant she'd had her meal.

There was no sign of Gillacoemgain, Fife, or Madelaine anywhere. I drifted through the kitchens. I saw many familiar faces as I grabbed bread, cheese, and a handful of dried meat then headed outside. Thora and I walked to the small creek that ran very close to the castle. I sat eating my breakfast, tossing the bits of dried meat to Thora as I watched fish dart through the water.

The air smelled fresh and clean. A soft wind blew across the hills and down the valley, carrying with it the scents of pine and damp grass. I closed my eyes and let the sun warm my body. Thora waded into the water and stood snapping at the fish and turning over rocks with her nose and paws.

I lay back in the grass and stared up at the sky. Thin wisps of clouds adorned the periwinkle blue sky.

My thoughts tumbled over themselves, each one begging to be heard first. I tried to focus on Gillacoemgain and my encounter—well, mine and the raven's—the night before, but no matter how hard I tried, my thoughts turned to Banquo. I wondered what, exactly, Epona had said to him that he'd given me up so easily.

Had Uald's words not comforted him? He could hardly deny his father and wait for a girl who might have been dead, or lost, or out of his reach in some fashion. He would have had to give in. And if he believed I was lost to the otherworld, he had no reason to wait. All my conjecture was pointless. In the end, I had lost the man I loved…that is, if Andraste was telling the truth. I could cast to Banquo and learn the answer for myself, but then what? Have my heart broken even further? And was it even safe to travel in such a manner while I was with child…no, children?

I sighed heavily and lay my hands on my stomach. Like Banquo, I would have to abandon my love. Gillacoemgain seemed likable. He would be the father of my children. I had to find a way to accept what I had lost. But as I thought of the children growing inside me, my mind flashed to Duncan, and the mist, and the rain. A tremor ran through my body.

"The scullery maids said to look for you here," a man's voice called, interrupting my thoughts. "I wondered if they jested, but here you are, lying like a fey thing amongst the grass."

I sat up and looked behind me. "Good morning, My Lord," I called to Gillacoemgain. Today he wore a black leather tunic that accented every curve of his chest. Goddess Mother, my head was a mess.

He sat down beside me. I broke off a piece of bread

and handed it to him as I eyed him over. He was even more handsome in the light of day. His eyes, which had seemed dark under the firelight in the hall, were actually an unusual gold-green color. And his hair picked up hints of gold, with a few strands of white, under the sunlight.

It seemed that he, too, was surveying me.

He smiled then stroked my hair. "It shines blue in the sunlight, the same shade as your gown."

"Madelaine always called me Corbie partially on account of that reason. My feathers shimmer," I said with a smile.

Gillacoemgain laughed. "Corbie? I like that. So tell me, Corbie, are there any fish in there?"

"Yes, and they are driving Thora mad," I replied.

Upon hearing her name, Thora looked up at me and wagged her tail.

Gillacoemgain tossed the hunk of bread I'd given him to her.

Thora, who never missed a meal, caught it like a marksman.

"You've found the best way to win her heart," I said with a laugh.

Gillacoemgain reached out and gently touched my chin. "And what about yours?"

"I...I must thank you for last evening. You were very gentle. It means so much," I whispered in truth. Through the raven's eyes, I had seen and felt him. He'd been passionate, but tender. Maybe next time, I could come to him as Gruoch. Maybe it would be safe.

"My lovely wife," he whispered then pulled me into a soft kiss. His lips were warm and soft, the stubble of a new beard scratching my skin.

"Shall we go back?" I asked after we finally let one another go.

Gillacoemgain nodded. Taking my hand in his, he led me across the grassy field. As I felt him beside me, towering over me, I realized that his presence made me feel…safe. It was an odd feeling, all things considered.

When we reached the castle gate, Madelaine was waiting for us. Gillacoemgain kissed my hand, bowed to Madelaine, then let me go.

"I'll meet you inside," he said then left me with my aunt.

"Well," Madelaine said with a chuckle, "this is unexpected."

I shrugged. How could I explain to her what I didn't understand myself?

Madelaine turned, and we headed into the castle. "My husband was informed of your late-night wandering."

"And did it trouble him?"

She laughed. "No. All was found…in order."

"Of course," I replied, trying to hide the disgust in my voice.

"I'm glad you like him. I know this is difficult, but

you are strong. I see you trying to make the best of it. I'm proud of you. You will do well in Moray."

"I hope so."

"Moray…you will be the queen of the old kingdom of Gododdin. Would your father have lived to see this day."

"Would my father have lived."

"These are strange times. Malcolm's health is waning, and Prince Duncan is unpopular. Your husband is an ambitious man. There may yet be a greater crown in your future. Malcolm has positioned Gillacoemgain to be an ally to that pompous boy, but Moray is not the kind of man who would follow a puppet on the throne. Watch your husband well. Guide him. He would need strong support behind him for any such bid, but a wife has her husband's ear more than any council."

A smile slipped across my face as I imagined Gillacoemgain putting an ax through Duncan's head.

"We shall see," I replied.

"What else can we do?" Madelaine said with a smile. "Now, come. Your farewell breakfast waits. You leave for Moray this afternoon."

"So soon?"

"He didn't tell you?"

No, he was too busy kissing me. "No."

"He needs to return. And you, my love, will go with him. You'll wed when you reach Moray."

"You're not coming?"

"The travel…it's not safe. And Fife is old," she said with a laugh.

"Then it will be goodbye again," I replied.

"Just for now."

I nodded. If I did as I'd promised, made good on my word to Epona, I would be back soon.

CHAPTER EIGHT

*T*he farewell feast for Gillacoemgain and me seemed almost surreal. How many times had I sat in the feasting hall under Alister's watch wishing I could disappear, hating everyone in the room save Madelaine and Tavis, hoping Alister would die? The scene that morning was quite different.

I sat sipping water and eating freshly baked cakes while I listened to Fife share funny stories. Madelaine laughed happily, her voice ringing through the chamber. A harper played softly in the corner.

"She never gets too far from you," Gillacoemgain said, playing with Thora's ears. Thora had planted herself between Gillacoemgain and me at the table. I'd noticed Gillacoemgain feeding her scraps all through breakfast. Thora responded to his playful toying by licking his hand. Thora usually had a very good sense of people. If

Gillacoemgain was the murdering warlord everyone said he was, why had Thora taken to him already?

"No, especially not when there's food to be had," I replied.

Gillacoemgain smiled and pulled a dagger from his belt. It was a lovely piece of weaponry with a golden pommel. He cut a chunk of meat from the wild boar sitting on the table before us and tossed it to Thora who wagged her tail happily.

"Where did you get her?"

"Foundling."

"Hmm," Gillacoemgain considered, looking into Thora's face. "I've never seen a dog quite like her before."

"My late uncle's priest threatened to drown her, accused her of being fey."

Gillacoemgain shook his head. "Fool," he muttered then leaned back in his chair. "Scotland is swarming with foolish men." Gillacoemgain sighed heavily. "Fife seems the type to enjoy lingering long over breakfast, but I've many things that need my attention in Moray. Would you mind too much if I ask you to get ready to depart?"

"Not at all. I have little patience with such courtly pleasantries."

Gillacoemgain smiled at me then set his hand on my shoulder. "Then we shall get along very well, Boite's daughter." He rose and crossed the room to talk to

Madelaine's husband, who was helping himself to his fourth serving that morning.

As the two men exchanged words, Madelaine rose and came to me.

"I'll help you dress in your riding clothes," she told me.

Together, we headed upstairs. I removed my courtly gown and slipped on a long tunic and a pair of riding breeches, strapping Uald's gift around my waist. In no time, I was ready to leave, my belongings already bundled onto the pack horses.

I met Gillacoemgain and his men outside.

Tavis waited with Kelpie.

"Now, that's a sight I don't think I've seen before," Gillacoemgain said as he eyed me wearing the sword. "This nunnery of yours...are you sure you didn't travel to the isle of Scáthach for training as a shieldmaiden?"

Tavis chuckled but said nothing.

"I was told all women in Moray were armed. Just trying to fit in," I replied as I mounted Kelpie. I reined in beside Gillacoemgain.

"A rose trying to fit in amongst weeds? I think not... Corbie," Gillacoemgain said with a smile.

Madelaine laughed at that. "Corbie. It does fit her well, doesn't it? Take good care of my little raven," she told Gillacoemgain.

"My Lady, nothing would make me happier," he

replied, and something in his expression told me he was being honest.

In spite of myself, I smiled. Life alongside Alister had led me to believe most courtly men were cruel. Duncan had proven that the world was still full of evil men. But Gillacoemgain, despite the rumors that surrounded him, had offered me some small hope. Perhaps the world was simply a mix of good and evil. Perhaps *people* were simply a mix of good and evil. And me, who had killed, what was I?

Thora trotted over to Kelpie and looked up at me expectantly.

"It's a long walk," I told her.

She simply wagged her tail.

Madelaine laughed then took my hand. "Be well, my little love. I grow weary of saying good-bye to you."

"And me to you. But I think I leave you in good hands," I said then lowered my voice. "Will Tavis stay at your side?"

Madelaine nodded. "I cannot live without him," she replied. "Be safe, and come back to me soon."

"I will," I told her, waved farewell to Tavis, then turned to Gillacoemgain and nodded.

"Lady Madelaine," Gillacoemgain said politely, inclining his head to my aunt. He then whistled to his men, and the party headed out.

*I*t was a long ride from Madelaine's keep to the castle at Cawdor. Riding was something I always loved. After the darkness of Ynes Verleath, to be amongst the green again was sheer delight. Many times, as we passed through dense forests, when the smell of loam and pine was strong, I thought of Sid. Had she been with me, all of this would have been so much easier. But Sid was not meant for the world outside the coven. Her faerie ways no longer belonged in the realm of men. Despite our separation, however, I knew I was soul-bound to Sid. The world was not done with us yet.

"Look there," Gillacoemgain said, pointing as we passed through an ancient forest. The trees there, mainly oaks loaded with bunches of mistletoe, loomed overhead.

I followed his gaze to see a mound amongst the trees. I shook away the memory of Banquo that was trying to insist itself on the moment.

"Fairy mound," Gillacoemgain said. "They say the great warrior queen Cartimandua and her druid advisor are buried within."

"Cartimandua?" the name struck my memory hard, but I shook my head.

"Cartimandua, Queen of the Brigantes," Gillacoemgain replied. "My mother loved history. She was proud that Moray watched over Cartimandua's bones and that of the druid who served her. This area was, and *still* is, partial toward the old gods, the old ways. You spent many years in the nunnery yet your father—"

"I am my father's daughter," I told Gillacoemgain. "And we all serve the gods, no matter their names."

"The people of Moray will be pleased to hear their lady is so wise."

"Would all in the kingdom were so wise," I replied. If Gillacoemgain did take hope to the throne, I would be able to directly influence the incursion of the Christian faith in Scotland. All people should be able to worship the way they wished. The Christians would not have it so. At Gillacoemgain's side, I could truly do good for those who held fast to the old ways. And the moment the idea struck me, I remembered what Andraste had said. Gruoch was needed in the real world. Was this why? "And what of Gillacoemgain? What gods do you serve?" I asked him.

"I serve Scotland."

I nodded. "Then serve her we shall."

Gillacoemgain raised an eyebrow at me. "In all things?"

"As the gods decree."

Gillacoemgain laughed. "I think the gods decreed us to be together…not just King Malcolm."

"Who is he compared to the gods?"

"Nothing," Gillacoemgain said.

I loved his answer. "Indeed," I replied.

We rode throughout the day. That night we made

camp along a stream deep in the woods. I could see from the way Gillacoemgain's men were eyeing me that they were wondering how I would take to sleeping outdoors. Thus far, despite multiple offers to stop and rest, I hadn't asked for any special treatment. This had, it seemed, won me some respect.

When the men set about preparing a tent for me, however, I intervened.

"No need, lads," I told them. "I can sleep under the stars the same as you."

"No, My Lady," one of the soldiers replied. "It's no bother. We wouldn't want a fine lady like you sleeping on the cold ground."

"My dog does a good job keeping me warm," I replied. "And there is always the Mormaer," I replied with a wink.

He laughed.

Overhearing the conversation, Fergus, who was never far from Gillacoemgain, stepped in. "It's no trouble, Lady Gruoch." He turned to the soldier, "See to it."

The soldier got back to work.

"Gillacoemgain wouldn't have it, Lady," Fergus told me.

Of course. It was for my husband to decide, wasn't it? I said nothing but instead went to work building up one of the campfires. Gillacoemgain, busy organizing his men, didn't notice. By the time he did finally find me, the small flame was already growing cheerfully.

"Corbie? Did you…" he looked from the fire to me and back again.

I shrugged. "I was cold."

He laughed then sat down beside me at the fire. "Well arranged," he said, looking into the flames. "Will make lots of heat and little smoke. Did you learn how to build a fire at the nunnery as well?" And this time, I heard the suspicion in his voice. If Gillacoemgain knew about the old gods, did that mean he also knew about the secret covens? Epona had said there were nine such covens spread about the land. As Mormaer of Moray, did he know of other such places?

I shrugged.

"May I?" he asked then, glancing down at my sword.

I nodded and pulled Uald's gift from the scabbard and handed the blade to him.

Gillacoemgain gripped the pommel, felt the sword's balance, then gave the blade a wave. "This is divine craftsmanship. Who gave it to you?"

"A woman, a smith, actually, who is close to Madelaine and me." How could I explain Uald to Gillacoemgain?

"Scáthach, I presume?" Gillacoemgain smiled. "You've some interesting acquaintances, Lady Corbie."

If only he knew.

Gillacoemgain handed the sword back to me. "Perhaps you can convince her to forge a blade for me."

"I think she would like you. She might consider it. That is a fine dagger you wear on your belt as well."

Gillacoemgain pulled off the dagger and handed it to me. The dagger was very old but well-made. There was a strange flower symbol on the pommel. It looked Pictish.

"It's lovely." I handed it back to him.

"It comes with a long story. It will suffice for now to say it has been in my family for a long time."

I nodded, eyeing the dagger once more. The craftsmanship was superb. It reminded me of the torcs from Ynes Verleath. Where had Gillacoemgain found such an ancient piece of weaponry?

Gillacoemgain motioned to the nearby tent. "Your lodging is prepared, whenever you're ready."

"I'll stay under the stars a bit more."

"We are here amongst my men only. Perhaps… perhaps I can join you this evening?"

My stomach knotted. "Of course," I whispered.

It was then that one of Gillacoemgain's men pulled out his pipes and played a tune. The sweet melody washed over the forest. We ate a meager meal as the men talked and the piper played. Soon, the gathering dispersed, and the men took their rest, lying down beside the fire.

Taking my hand, Gillacoemgain led me to the tent. The men, I noticed, paid their Mormaer no mind. At least, they pretended not to notice.

Inside, they had laid a bear fur on the ground and

heaped it with blankets. Once inside, Gillacoemgain embraced me gently then pulled me into a kiss. His mouth tasted of wine, his lips soft and warm. I caught that sweet scent of lavender and cedar once more. I fell into the kiss and allowed myself to be with him. Despite the rumors, he seemed to be a good man. And if he wasn't, then the raven knew what to do.

"Corbie," he whispered, stroking my long hair.

Gently, he undid the laces on the back of my dress then pulled it over my head. I slid off my riding breeches then stood naked before him. I shoved away all thoughts of Banquo and of Duncan. I had to. I closed the lid on those feelings and tried to be there, only with Gillacoemgain, in that moment. Gillacoemgain slid off his clothes then gently laid me down. My hands danced across his strong back. I then stroked his arms, feeling his muscles, his body, as he drizzled kisses down my neck. He then gently kissed my nipples while his hands stroked my body.

In spite of the violence I had faced, in spite of everything, my body responded eagerly to him. Any woman would have found him attractive. I knew that my mind was my enemy so I tried to rule myself. One day, Duncan would pay for what he'd done. In the meantime, I would give Moray an heir and take control over my heart and mind once more. I closed down the thoughts tripping over themselves and emptied my head. I let myself feel his flesh and take what pleasure I could.

He entered me gently, still careful with his young bride. The sensation sent me spinning, and my mind went to Banquo. I closed my eyes and shut away the thought. I tried to breathe in Gillacoemgain, to honor and respect the spirit inside him. The only problem was, the spirit within me wanted only one man. Despite my best effort, I made love to Gillacoemgain while dreaming of Banquo, knowing my true love's soul was lost to me.

CHAPTER NINE

*W*e arrived the next morning at the ancient fortress of Cawdor. The keep, built upon the site of an old Pictish stronghold, was constructed of pale gray stone. We rode our horses through the gate to the ward.

"Welcome home, Lady Gruoch," Fergus said as he helped me dismount.

Gillacoemgain's household rushed outside to meet us, and the scene soon turned into a busy flurry of activity as horses were led away to the stables, servants headed inside with my belongings, and news was delivered.

A small man wearing a red tunic came to Gillacoemgain's side and buzzed about him like a bee. He unloaded all manner of information on the Mormaer as soon as Gillacoemgain. "Enough, Artos. I must see to my wife," he said then turned me. "Gruoch, this is Artos. He is my counselor here at Cawdor."

"Lady Gruoch." The man bowed deeply.

The raven eyed him and decided she did not like this man.

"Artos."

"Corbie, we've employed a maid for you," Gilla-coemgain said then, waving over a red-haired woman who had been amongst the other members of the household. "This is Ute."

"My Lady," she said, dropping into a curtsey.

"Ute, please take the Lady of Moray to my chamber and get her settled in," he told the girl then turned to me. "I must go to council now, but I will come as soon as I can," he said softly then kissed me on the forehead. "Welcome home, my bride."

"Thank you," I said, squeezing his hand in farewell.

"This way, My Lady," Ute said, motioning for me to follow her.

I whistled to Thora, who came padding along behind us.

"It's an honor to meet you, Lady Gruoch. To think, you are the niece of King Malcolm. It is my pleasure to serve you."

"Thank you, Ute," I replied. "But please, no formalities between us. Let us be friends."

Ute smiled. "Thank you, My L—thank you, Gruoch."

I was led through the castle, which was not unlike

Madelaine's keep, to a bed chamber with a good view of the ward. The room looked as though it had been freshly spruced up for Gillacoemgain and me. I could smell the scent of freshly washed linens and new straw. From the look of the stones, the floors and walls had recently been scrubbed. A fire burned, driving off the last of the chill in the spring air. I sat down on the bed, realizing then that I was exhausted. The road had been long, and my body ached.

"Ute, I think I shall take some rest," I told the girl.

"Of course."

I looked down at Thora. "This is Thora. She is dear to me. Will you see that she has something to eat?"

Ute smiled down at Thora. "Well, bonnie girl, how about a bone?"

Thora barked, which made Ute laugh.

"Would you like some help getting undressed? The Mormaer had some things brought for you. You'll find all manner of dresses in the trunk," she said, motioning to a wood chest.

I shook my head. Suddenly, I felt quite dizzy.

"No, thank you."

"Take your rest. I won't wake you unless the Mormaer asks for you," she said then left.

Sighing deeply, I crossed the room and opened the chest. Gillacoemgain and Madelaine, it seemed, liked the idea of seeing me in court gowns. Inside I saw red, green, and blue gowns trimmed with fine lace and embroidery.

I pulled out a simple nightdress. Pulling off my riding gear, I slipped on the gown and lay down. I was a bride. And soon, I would be a mother. Taking one step out of Ynes Verleath had changed my entire life.

*U*te woke me later that evening and helped me bathe and dress for dinner. I had already grown tired of the constant grooming. I pulled on the red gown, brushing out my long, dark hair, and then followed Ute to the dining hall where I was seated beside a very tired-looking Gillacoemgain. He smiled as best he could, but I could see that the ride, and the onslaught of news, had exhausted him. I was introduced to the Mormaers of Buchan and Mar and people talked of trade and of Thorfinn of Orkney. I listened.

King Malcolm favored Gillacoemgain to control the north over Thorfinn or Macbeth. The king questioned Thorfinn's relationship with Norway and Macbeth's relationship with Thorfinn. My marriage to Gillacoemgain was the king's way of sending a clear message to any contenders that the king wanted Gillacoemgain to be the Lord of the North, as the Mormaer of Moray was generally considered. But if Gillacoemgain wanted to take control of Thorfinn's lands, now was the time. These were things everyone knew, and everyone was waiting to see what Gillacoemgain would do. They also seemed to be wondering what, if anything, Gillacoemgain and King Malcolm had secretly planned. Gillacoemgain, however, only seemed to want to get married and think things through; at least that was my observation. And that night, I was certain, the only thing Gillacoemgain wanted was sleep.

"My Lord looks weary," I whispered in his ear when those closest to us had turned their attention away.

"I've spent too long riding to hear all manner of news at once, but that is the nature of things for me," he said, sipping a concoction of warm, honey-sweetened herbs.

"Will you have counsel all night or will you rest?"

"More hereafter, I'm afraid. Malcolm sent a priest north to wed us. He arrived a while ago but is sleeping. I hope you will forgive me, but I have not planned a lavish wedding. Moray's money has been spent to ensure I keep my place here."

"I need no trappings to wed," I replied.

Gillacoemgain laughed. "If Malcolm had not offered your hand, Corbie, I would have come for you myself."

My heart fluttered open. "Thank you."

Gillacoemgain smiled and stroked my cheek.

I looked at Gillacoemgain, and for a brief moment, I saw a flash of red on his face, a glow like he was beside a fire. Strange. I closed my eyes, forcing the image away.

"Corbie?" he whispered. "Are you all right?

"I'm fine," I said, pulling myself back together. It was nothing more than a shadow, a strange trick of the light.

"The ride was too much for you and the talk grows weary. Why don't you rest?"

"Not yet. Will you come to our chamber tonight?"

Gillacoemgain sighed tiredly. "I must meet with Buchan and Mar. There is much to consider."

"Will it come to war then?"

"So it seems. The last of those who support Thorfinn must be subdued."

"There is no way to bring him to an accord?"

Gillacoemgain shook his head. "The Viking thinks his line rules the north. He's wrong. I will not have our children's birthright threatened. I will stamp him out and those who support him."

"Has he much support?"

"Enough to give me a problem, but I have Malcolm."

Rather, I thought, Malcolm had Gillacoemgain, but I didn't say so.

He put his arm around me then and pulled me close. "What do you think of my castle?"

"I've seen little more than our chamber. But I love the ward, the green space inside the castle walls."

"There is another garden," Gillacoemgain said distractedly, "but it's unused. The soil may be bad there," he said, shifting in his seat. He sighed. "When this business is done, we'll go out and hunt together, my birds and your dog. They'll make a great team."

"Birds?"

"My falcons," he said, his eyes sparkling with buried joy.

"I look forward to those quiet days."

"As do I," Gillacoemgain said, stroking my hair, "as do I."

CHAPTER TEN

*D*espite Gillacoemgain's desire for quiet, rest, and a peaceful life, there was no sign of it on the horizon. I waited up for him that night, but he never came to our chamber.

The following morning, I learned from Ute that the men had been in counsel all night. Riders had been coming in and out of Cawdor at all hours. From the viewpoint above the ward, I saw messengers rushing in and out of the castle. Moray was a busy place. Madelaine's castle had lived in a quiet lull. Nothing happened saved the grotesque antics of Alister. In Moray, things were very different. The north, it seemed, was bracing for conflict.

Gillacoemgain arrived midday, however, with news.

"Corbie?" he called, rapping on the chamber door. He looked very pale. Dark rings had formed under his eyes.

"Gillacoemgain? You look miserable," I said, crossing the room to take his hand.

"It's nothing," he said, dismissing his obvious fatigue. "I spoke with the priest this morning. He can perform the nuptials today," he said then added, "I have to say, he took the news that there wasn't a lavish event planned worse than the bride."

"I hope you told him so."

"I did," Gillacoemgain said with a laugh. "I suspect he's used to women of southern stock. Royal girls do have a reputation for demanding pageantry."

"Should I stamp my foot and demand heaps of jewels?" I asked playfully. "After all, I've come with quite a dowry."

"If you want, but I don't have any jewels to give you. I do have something, though," he said and crossed the room to his trunk. From within, he pulled out a bundle wrapped in cloth and set it on the bed. "I had this made for you."

Curious, I opened the package. Inside I found a stunning violet-colored gown trimmed with silver embroidery. "How did you know? The colors…"

"I didn't, but there is a woman in Nairn who my sister trusted to make her gowns. I asked the dressmaker to sew something for you. Do you like it?"

"It's beautiful," I said, stunned that Gillacoemgain had thought to ensure I had something special to wear. But his words caught my attention. I hadn't known he had a sister. For a fleeting moment, I envisioned a female friend for myself, a co-conspirator in mischief and someone to be with me through my pregnancy.

"We've set the time of the nuptials at dusk. Does that suit you?"

"Yes," I said, stroking my hand across the lovely fabric. "I didn't know you had a sister."

Gillacoemgain stiffened, and it felt as if the air around us grew cold. "Had. She was…she's dead."

I could feel all the sharp edges around the topic so I let it go. As fleeting as my dream had come, it vanished just as quickly. "A wedding at dusk," I said gently, thinking not only of the lovely sunset hues but also how weddings after midday were said to bring bad luck.

"Yes, I know, ten people have already told me that the time of day is ill-omened, but I must leave soon, and I want our marriage confirmed. And I want to join my wife in bed," he said, wrapping his arms around me.

I let go of everything in that moment and felt him, just him. I owed it to both of us to try to make it work.

"Corbie. My raven bride," he said then kissed the back of my head. "I'll see you at dusk."

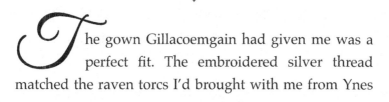

*T*he gown Gillacoemgain had given me was a perfect fit. The embroidered silver thread matched the raven torcs I'd brought with me from Ynes

Verleath. I slid on the amulet and bracelets. They glimmered in the fading sunlight.

"You look so beautiful," Ute said as she wound my hair with colorful ribbons, inserting violets, small white flowers, and bits of ivy.

I strung a piece of matching ribbon around Thora's neck, making Ute laugh and Thora look at me like I was mad.

"What? You look festive," I told Thora, who simply wagged her tail.

There was a knock on the door.

"They are ready for you, My Lady," Artos called from the other side of the door.

"I don't like that man," Ute told me in a whisper. "None of the servants do."

I, too, sensed the danger on Artos. I nodded.

"Keep your head still or all the flowers will fall out," Ute told me with a giggle.

Artos waited just outside the chamber. "This way," he said, leading us down the hallway toward a part of the castle I'd never been in before. The hallways looked a bit unused, everything dusty.

"What is this place? Visitor's quarters?" I asked Artos.

He shook his head. "This was the wing Lord Findelach resided in before his falling out with Gillacoemgain. Lord Findelach went to Inverness afterward. This area is unused now, but the only chapel in the castle is here."

"Was Findelach a Christian?" It surprised me to think that Gillacoemgain, who seemed so ambivalent about religion, had a pious brother...one that Gillacoemgain had murdered.

"In his way," Artos replied but said nothing more.

We wound down the stairs to a small courtyard, a garden really, outside the chapel. There, apple trees bloomed with lovely white blossoms. They perfumed the air. Benches and even some small fountains decorated the space. At once, I noticed a fairy ring growing amongst the green. Was this the garden Gillacoemgain had mentioned? If it was, then the soil was not only good but touched with magic. The place was lovely. Torches had been lit all along the pathway from the main castle corridor to the small stone building at the other side of the courtyard. Terraces from the chambers around the garden looked out at the green space. This area of the castle must have once been very beautiful. Firelight shimmered brilliantly against the burning colors of the sunset. The sky, streaked ruby red and deep purple, was alive with fire.

Several nicely dressed lords and ladies, many of whom I had not yet met, waited at the door. They bowed when I drew near.

"My Lady," Fergus said, taking my arm. "The Lord of Mar has offered to escort you in."

I smiled at Fergus, who had shaved and bathed for the wedding. "Very well," I replied, and Fergus led me to the Lord whom I'd met briefly at dinner the evening before.

"Lady Gruoch," the Lord of Mar said as he took my arm. He was an older gentleman with thinning silver hair and a lanky frame. He too was dressed in fine clothes, wearing the colored cloth of Mar. "I'm so pleased to see you wed. Never fear, my girl," he said, patting my hand, "Gillacoemgain is a reliable man. Don't let the rumors dissuade you. That business with Findelach never made sense to me."

"Why not?"

"Gillacoemgain was always a quiet, thoughtful young man. Seemed like he'd rather hunt boars than go to war. Findelach was quite different; ambitious, arrogant, pious. We wouldn't have been surprised if it had been him. Please forgive me. We shouldn't speak of such things at your nuptials. I just hoped to calm any nerves you might have. Would that your father could have seen this day, lass. Did you know I knew him? And your mother? I was there when we brought Emer back from Ireland. All us lads could do was stare at your mother. She was the loveliest thing I'd ever seen…save you in this moment. You are quite a vision."

"Thank you, My Lord." I was taken aback to find my mother's and father's name and presence once more as I wed. It had never occurred to me that anyone would remember my mother.

"You look much like her," he continued then, "except you've got your father's coloring. Moray is a lucky man. Lovely Emer," he said as we walked up the steps into the chapel. "We were all so jealous of your father. She had eyes only for him. Did you know she could play the harp? On the way back from Ireland, she strummed the harp and sang to us. No idea what she was singing about, but her voice sounded like a dove," he said.

When we stepped into the church, Mar became silent, which seemed to be difficult for him. The little chapel was lit by candlelight. The light cast long shadows on the statues of Christian saints sitting in alcoves along the walls. The priest King Malcolm had sent from Edinburgh was heavily robed, heavily jeweled, and had flabby flesh hanging under his chin.

The priest motioned for me to come forward as a small lad who accompanied him, perhaps no more than eight years of age, began singing in Latin. The small chapel filled with the child's dulcet tones.

Mar led me to Gillacoemgain, who looked very handsome in a soft gray shirt with the belted blue and green plaid of Moray around his waist and chest, clasped with a silver tartan pin. Like most highlanders, he wore no leggings, just his black leather boots. He wore a matching feathered cap.

Mar passed my hand to Gillacoemgain. We turned then and gave our attention to King Malcolm's priest.

The priest then began the ceremony in Latin. While Epona had taught me well, I was only half-interested in following what the priest said. In essence, under the eyes of God and King, I now belonged to Moray. It mattered little what the actual words were.

I looked at Gillacoemgain out of the corner of my eye. He, too, looked mildly annoyed, but he was trying not to show it. He could not help but crack a smile when, despite Ute's whispered protests, Thora came forward to join us. She sat at my side, looking from Gillacoemgain to me. I giggled but tried to keep my composure.

A moment later, Ute convinced Thora to come to her. I noticed then that a small lad, one of the stable boys, led Thora away from the chapel. She jumped around the boy excitedly.

My attention lost, I was surprised when the priest motioned to Gillacoemgain.

Gillacoemgain, who was still choking back a laugh, took a bundle of Moray tartan from Fergus. Then, regaining his composure, he wound the fabric around me.

"By Christ, and with the blessing of King Malcolm of Scotland, I pronounce Gruoch, daughter of Boite of the line MacAlpin and Gillacoemgain, Mormaer of Moray, bound as one."

Gillacoemgain took my hand, and we turned to face the assembled crowd.

The happy group cheered, and Gillacoemgain planted a quick kiss on my lips.

"How beautiful you look," Gillacoemgain said, pulling me close to him. "Especially in the cloth of Moray!"

"Many thanks, my husband. You, too, are a sight! Though I do hope you brought an extra strip or two of cloth?"

"What for?"

"For Thora, of course," I replied, making those standing close to us laugh.

"Malcolm told me 'you cannot have the bride unless you take her dog as well,'" he joked.

The crowd laughed.

"Come, friends. Let's dine," Gillacoemgain called and pipers, who'd been waiting outside the chapel, began to play. They led the small group through the courtyard back to the main castle where a royal supper, drink, music, and all manner of sweets awaited the small crowd.

The dinner was not lavish by any courtly standard, but I noticed that the good wine had been brought out, ale was plentiful, and two deer, hens, and even a boar had been roasted for the event. The music was merry and everyone seemed joyful. Most of the local lords and ladies were in attendance, as were many of the local clan leaders. That night, we dined and toasted our matrimony. And that night, when Gillacoemgain joined me in bed, I let him into my heart.

"Love does not come easy to a man like me," Gillacoemgain whispered in my ear, "but you've quite won me."

The sharp edges around my heart softened. "It is the same for me," I replied.

And that night, when I made love to my husband, my mind didn't wander. That night, Gruoch wed Gillacoemgain and became the Lady of Moray. That night, a woman took her new husband. And the raven was nowhere to be seen.

CHAPTER ELEVEN

The week following the wedding, Gillacoemgain left. Before his departure, however, I began making plans to visit the local families. When Gillacoemgain caught wind of my plans, however, he intervened.

"I don't understand," he told me as he prepared for his departure. I helped him slide his riding tunic over his head, lacing up the sides as he pulled on his gloves. "Why do you want to ride out? There is more than enough to keep you busy here in Cawdor. Mind the castle or do nothing at all, it's up to you."

"I don't like to be locked up in the keep. The castle makes me weary. I am the Lady of Moray. I want to meet her people."

Using his teeth, Gillacoemgain attempted to tighten the laces on his wrist.

"Here, My Lord," I said, taking his hand. "You have a wife now who can help with that," I added with a smile.

Gillacoemgain reached out and touched my chin. "Stay inside, little Corbie. War is brewing, and you are a valuable prize. You are my bride, and I will protect you, but your pretty head would make for a rich ransom."

"Ransom? And who would abduct me?"

"More forces than I can name."

"I'll take a guard with me. It will be safe, and I have my sword."

Gillacoemgain smiled lightly, but I saw irritation growing behind his eyes. "Stay in the castle. Moray's people, and their problems, will make their way to you. You are my wife. I want you safe. I'll leave Artos here to assist you. Your voice is the law, but he knows my will, so follow his suggestions."

"My Lord, I do wish you would let me ride out to see the people. Even if just briefly—"

"Enough! Do as I ask, no more. You have a whole castle to run. Is that not enough?"

I opened my mouth to protest, but Gillacoemgain set a soft kiss on my forehead.

"I know you are strong. And you are no doubt stubborn, given your blood, but please stay safe while I'm away. I cannot go into battle worried about you. When I return, we shall ride all day if it pleases you."

I studied the man. It felt odd to have someone look after me. Madelaine, of course, had mothered me, loved me. I wasn't sure if I should take Gillacoemgain's concern as adorable or suffocating. He was no Alister, so I was not running to the woods for a scant breath of freedom as Madelaine had, but Banquo would never have penned me in. And no one dares cage the raven. I felt confused.

"All right," I said hesitantly.

Once more he kissed me on the forehead, and we headed outside.

Fergus waited with Gillacoemgain's horse in the castle ward. The Mormaer mounted his steed.

"How long?" I asked Gillacoemgain.

"First we'll silence Lochaber and Echmarcach of the isles. Then, we'll see what Thorfinn does."

"Lochaber?" I asked in alarm. The word came out of my mouth with more emotion than was seeming. "I...I knew a lass from there," I lied.

"If I can convince the new young lord of Lochaber to see reason, war will not reach her doorstep," Gillacoemgain said.

"Lochaber's loyalty blows with the wind. Let's see if the son is any brighter than the father was. No doubt word of your marriage has reached him. Perhaps Malcolm's niece in your bed will keep him quiet," Fergus said.

"We'll see. Thorfinn," Gillacoemgain spat, "is busy stirring the beehive. I'll have that Viking's heart on the spit if it's the last thing I do," he said then turned back to me. "May the gods watch over you, little raven," he told me then.

My body shaking, I nodded. "Farewell, Gillacoemgain. May the Morrigu ride with you."

Fergus laughed. "Now that's a blessing I'd take."

Gillacoemgain nodded to me then turned and rode out of the castle.

I watched as they rode off to confront…Banquo. And what if Banquo didn't see reason? What if…I couldn't think of it. I swooned.

Ute came up beside me. She reached out to steady me. "Gruoch? Are you all right? Come inside. You're pale as milk. I'd swear you are already with child. And with a strapping husband like our Mormaer, it won't be long if you aren't already pregnant."

"Yes," I said absently, mindful of how Ute's eyes were glued to Gillacoemgain's shape as he rode away. "Yes, he is my husband," I said, feeling annoyed. I shook Ute's hand off and headed back into the castle.

"Gruo—My Lady?" she called.

"I'll send for you if I need you," I replied then headed back to my chamber. Seized with a sudden and fierce desire to know, beyond all shadow of a doubt, I barred the door to my chamber and closed the heavy drapes, shutting out all light.

I opened my bags and pulled out all manner of herbs. Stoking the fire, I dashed the herbs on the flames. The room filled with smoke. I sat before the fire and stared into the small cauldron hanging there.

Cerridwen of the cauldron.

Raven goddess.

Mother.

Queen.

Come to me.

I closed my eyes and inhaled deeply. The room was filled with the scent of heady white sage. Once my spirit loosened from my body, I opened my eyes and stared into the cauldron.

Banquo.

Banquo.

The water in the cauldron stirred and soon I saw a rocky coastline. The moment I saw it, my spirit leapt into the scene. I was the raven once more.

Wind rushed against my face, and the sound of my raven's wings beating in the air made my heart quicken. I dived, feeling the rush of the wind, smelling the sea air. With my sharp raven eyes, I looked down the coastline. Ahead, I saw a bay wherein at least a dozen ships were preparing to set sail. I flew toward the scene. Soldiers boarded ships as a party on land made their good-byes.

From above, I circled the scene. Something, someone, glimmered silver amongst the assembled crowd. I swooped lower to see.

There he was.

Banquo.

Keeping a distance, I landed on a dead tree nearby and watched as my husband, my *real* husband, embraced a man I had seen once before. Before Banquo stood the same blond-haired giant who had saved my raven-headed man in battle. Banquo said something to him that I couldn't quite hear. The man laughed out loud.

"Jarl Thorfinn, we're ready for you," a soldier told the man.

Thorfinn. I eyed him closely. He seemed…merry. That was a surprise. Banquo embraced the Viking.

I studied Banquo closely. He looked older. Worry clouded his handsome features. The others would not have noticed, but I did. How handsome he was. How sweet and wonderful he was.

"Farewell!" I heard a lady call.

The raven turned and saw a woman come to stand beside Banquo, taking his hand in hers.

"My Lady of Lochaber," Thorfinn called cheerfully in reply, lifting his massive ax in salute, then headed with his men in the direction of the ships.

I could not take my eyes from her. She had dark hair and light eyes. In truth, she looked a bit like me. And in her arms, she held a small child.

She smiled up at Banquo.

Banquo sighed, buried his worries, then turned and smiled at her.

The raven could not bear it.

I shrieked loudly at them.

Banquo trembled then turned and faced me.

It was all true. He was allied with Thorfinn. He had wed another and had a child with her besides. He had forgotten me.

I opened my mouth to speak, to scream in anguish, but only the raven could call. She screeched in angry tones.

Banquo took a step toward me.

"Cerridwen?" he whispered.

I gasped then turned and fled. But I was overcome, suddenly, with the sensation that I was falling. And a moment later, I found myself lying on the stone floor beside the cold fire.

Unable to stop myself, I wept. Everything caught me then, and I dropped down into a dark oblivion. Sharp pains shot through my skull, and I felt my body shake and shake. I couldn't stop myself, no matter how hard I tried. The pain felt too real. It was too much. I shook and rocked until my body had worn itself out. After, I fell into a deep sleep. In that dream, I walked the deserted streets of Ynes Verleath in complete quiet and darkness. Nothing plagued my soul. I walked and walked, breathing in the deep scent of wisteria. I traveled down the crumbling hallways until I found myself at the cauldron terrace once more.

Andraste's familiar huddled shape sat near the fire.

"Andraste?" I asked.

But when the figure turned, it was the Morrigu.

Blood dripped from the corners of her mouth. "Wake up, and get to work," she snapped.

Startling me awake, I found myself lying still on the cold floor.

I rose and crossed the room, pulling away the window covers to discover it was already night.

The yard was empty save one small boy who was looking up at my window. When he saw me, he bowed then ran off to the stables.

I sat down on my bed and stared up at the moon shining in through the open casement.

"As you wish," I answered the bloody goddess.

CHAPTER TWELVE

"How many cases of wine this evening, Lady Gruoch?"

"What songs would you like to hear?"

"How many pheasants would you like roasted?"

In the weeks that followed, the "get to work" mandate made by the bloody goddess started to feel like a joke. I was, once more, back to the same dull lifestyle I had lived while growing up. Again, I was bound to the castle and the boring drudgery it wrought. How had Madelaine endured the unending tedium of running a household? But I did as Gillacoemgain asked, not just because he asked it, but because the quickening within me was starting to become more and more obvious. And along with it, I was suddenly taking with vomiting in the morning, dizzy spells, and heavy afternoon tiredness. The first three months, alone in the castle with no one but Ute for company, began to feel a lot like a replay of my time with Madelaine.

"My Lady is with child," Ute told me.

"Yes," I replied absently as I sat looking out the window.

"Have you sent word to the Mormaer?"

"No. I don't want anything to distract Gillacoemgain."

"But the news is joyful," Ute said, confused.

"Yes. And when he returns, I'll tell him. In the meantime, we'll say nothing. I won't have him worried about me, or his unborn child, while he's on the battlefield."

"Yes, My Lady."

Word had slowly returned that Gillacoemgain had, in fact, traveled to Lochaber. There he'd brought young Lord Banquo, who'd recently taken over power due to his father's death, into accord. Banquo, it seemed, was extremely good at deceptive diplomacy. Gillacoemgain, near as I had learned, had not discovered Banquo was in league with Thorfinn. Did I have an obligation to tell him? I wasn't sure. My emotions tumbled over themselves, and at times my head ached as much as my heart.

Rumors about the Thorfinn, blond-haired Viking, however, were easy to come by. As Jarl of Caithness and Orkney, Thorfinn should have bowed to the will of the Lord of Moray who was overlord of the north. But he held no allegiance to Gillacoemgain. The north was not at peace with the Mormaer of Moray, despite our marriage. In the hall, they whispered that Gillacoemgain was thought a cutthroat and usurper by those in the northern-most provinces. The people of Moray, however, seemed to respect him. Rumors abounded that Gillacoemgain's elder brother, Findelach, had been the man Thorfinn had rallied behind. For reasons I had not yet discovered, Gillacoemgain had murdered his brother. Findelach's son, Macbeth, was still held in watchful "fostering" under Malcolm, a condition that was little more than political imprisonment. My marriage to Gillacoemgain was intended to subdue the north, but it had only done so in halves.

One morning, I went to the council chamber where a number of people had gathered to have their complaints heard.

Artos, Gillacoemgain's advisor, attended to most of the small issues. By the time I arrived, only a few people remained, including a tearful scullery maid whom I found on her knees before Artos.

"My Lady," he said politely when I entered. While most of Gillacoemgain's household had welcomed me eagerly, Artos was an exception. Artos had a sharp tongue and an attitude that suggested he believed women had their place...subservient to men. It was an attitude I could not abide. That morning, already feeling out of sorts due to my growing stomach, worry over Gillacoemgain, and frustration with Banquo, I was in no mood for misogyny.

"What is the matter here?" I asked.

"My Lady of Moray," the girl said, who I recognized as part of our household, pleaded, looking desperate. "Please, will you hear me? Master Artos—"

"We need not bother her ladyship with petty issues. Take her away, and twenty lashes, as I have ordered."

The girl's eyes widened. She looked about frantically.

I motioned to the guards to hold.

"I will decide what I hear, Artos. What is it, lass?"

"She's a thief, My Lady," Artos injected.

"I didn't ask you," the raven snapped at him. "Go on," I added, turning to the girl.

"My Lady," the girl said, "please, I beg your forgiveness. My father's farm burned. My family has had but scraps to eat these many weeks, barely holding on with what I can bring home. My father is too old to hunt, and my husband was wounded in the fire. I...I took some extra food to my family. My boy, he's but a wee slip of a thing. He's caught the fever that is spreading amongst the children. If he—"

I raised my hand to stop her then turned to Artos.

"Did she explain the same to you?"

"She did," Artos said, puffing out his chest.

"And is it true, that their farm burned?"

"I...I don't know," Artos answered.

"Of course you don't," I told him then turned back to the girl. "Are you telling me the truth?"

"Yes, My Lady."

She was. The answer was plain on her face. I turned to Artos once more. "And the fever afflicting the children? Is there a fever in Moray?"

"I..." Artos began, "I'm not—" he began but someone from the crowd spoke up.

"There is, My Lady of Moray," one of the farmers called. "In Nairn, we've lost ten children already, and many more are ill."

"Do you have learned women in these parts to heal such ailments?" I asked the farmer.

"Not anymore," he said, flicking an eye at the collection of Christian petitioners waiting to be heard.

I turned to Artos. "We feed the hungry in Moray, sir. And if that was not the custom before my arrival, it is now."

"But My Lady."

"Artos, I want you to provide me with a full accounting of Moray's supplies when I return this evening."

"Return?"

"Yes," I said. I crossed the room and lifted the girl by the hand. "Go to the kitchens and take what you need for your family. What's your name?"

"Tira."

"Tira, my apologies for how you were treated in my house," I said then turned on Artos. "You are no longer permitted to hold public hearings on behalf of Moray. Busy yourself with papers and coins but not with people.

I'll let Gillacoemgain decide what to do with you when he returns."

"My Lady!"

"That is my word. Abide it," the raven spat.

"But My Lady…"

I turned then and fixed my eyes on him. I could feel my heart beating hard. The raven wanted to rip him to shreds. "Who was my father?"

"You…you are the daughter of Boite."

"And who is my uncle?"

Artos paled. "King Malcolm."

"I am no pampered lap dog, Artos. I'm made of the stuff from my father's line. You will not disobey the blood of MacAlpin."

"Yes, My Lady," he said, the blood completely drained from his face. He was shaking. He'd seen the raven and had feared it.

"You, sir," I said, waving to the farmer. "Has your case been heard?"

"No, My Lady."

"I shall hear it as we ride."

"Ride?" he replied.

"To Nairn," I answered, then looked down at the girl. "My maid shall bring you a tonic for your boy."

"Thank you, My Lady," she said, a relieved, and mildly shocked, expression on her face.

"Anyone else seeking the justice of Moray today?" I asked the assembled crowd.

One of the Christians stepped forward. "We've come to offer our services to your court, Lady Gruoch. We've traveled from the court of King Malcolm ready to serve you and the Mormaer of Moray."

I smiled as nicely as the raven would allow. "Please give these men supplies so they may travel back to my uncle, the king," I said, glancing back at Artos. "Their services are not required in Cawdor."

"But, My Lady, Cawdor doesn't have anyone from the holy brotherhood providing ministering to your household," one of the holy men protested.

"Correct," I replied. "Nor do we need any. Safe travels to you, gentleman," I replied, then turned to the farmer. "Your name, sir?"

"James, My Lady."

"Let me assemble my supplies and a guard, and we'll see what we can do about that fever."

The man looked stunned. "Many thanks, Lady Gruoch."

I nodded and headed back upstairs.

It was time to get busy.

CHAPTER THIRTEEN

"*My* Lady," Ute protested as I packed my box full of the medicines I'd brought with me from the coven, "the Mormaer wouldn't want you leaving the castle in your fragile condition."

"Fragile? What about me is fragile?" I retorted, annoyed, as I pulled out several small bottles and mixed a draft. I then applied some distilled oils to a salve. When I was done, I packaged both up and handed the bundle to Ute. "Take this to the lass, Tira, who Artos nearly had lashed. Tell her but two sips once a day of the draft, but to rub the oils on his chest and feet. If she sees no change in two nights, let me know and I'll go see the boy."

"My Lady, you are with child! You will risk the life of your unborn healing these children."

"No, I won't. I am learned in such craft, Ute. I know

how to handle medicines and sick people." Epona had taught me well. Now, at last, I had a chance to use my skills. While Gillacoemgain had asked me not to leave the castle, there was no way he expected me to sit at home for months on end. Surely, he would understand. I hoped.

I finished packing my boxes and then headed outside where a small guard, and the farmer, waited.

"We'll escort you, Lady Gruoch," one of the soldiers said. He was an older man, one of the more regular guards I saw roaming about the castle.

"Thank you, though I hardly expect trouble during an impromptu trip. But thank you, all the same."

"The Mormaer would have our skin if anything happened to you. He might have it anyway knowing we let you out of the castle," the man replied.

"Your name, sir?"

"Standish."

"Well, you can just tell the Mormaer there was no stopping me. That would be the truth," I said, winking at him. I then turned to James, the farmer who'd spoken up. "May I ride with you?"

Bemused, he smiled. "Of course, My Lady."

After I settled into the bench alongside the farmer, we headed out. Thora, who'd been playing with one of the stable boys, caught sight of me. Leaving the stick she'd been chasing behind, she ran to catch up.

"Almost missed an adventure," I told her.

She barked at me.

I looked back at the boy in the yard. I'd seen the lad a few times now. He was the one who'd lured Thora away at the wedding. I'd need to make an effort to seek out this child who'd won Thora's heart. I waved to him.

Grinning, the child waved back then ran off.

"You said you were waiting to have a case heard?" I asked James as we rode.

"I'm rather glad it's your ear I have on the matter, Lady Gruoch," he told me then. "My problem is one of matrimony. I want to wed the daughter of my neighbor, but he won't give her up without more of a bride price than I can afford to give. She's not his only child. He's got five daughters. I could win any other bride for a better price, but my heart won't have it. I love the girl."

"Then I shall speak to this man in exchange for your time today."

James laughed. "Old Douglas, what's he going to say to the King's niece?"

"Let's hope he says yes."

At that, James laughed.

We rode from Cawdor Castle a short distance toward the little village of Nairn on the Moray Firth. The sky was bright blue colored, stray clouds drifting overhead. The weather was warm. We rode for a while when the farmer guided his cart toward a small farmhouse. The little white building, the roof made of thatch, sat in a lush green field.

"There are three children here who have the fever, assuming they are still alive," James said, directing his cart toward the house.

A woman stepped outside the little cottage, wiping her hands on her long skirts. We stopped just before the door. She eyed the Moray men suspiciously.

"Afternoon, Flora," James said as he pulled the wagon to a stop. He got out then turned and offered me his hand.

"And what's this all about? Are those...are those the Mormaer's men?"

"They are," James answered, "and this is the Lady of Moray."

"You've brought the Lady of Moray to my house?" the woman said, and I could tell by the expression on her face that she hadn't really meant to say it out loud. "My Lady," she said, curtseying to me.

"Please," I replied, reaching out to take her by the elbow. "James says your children have taken ill with fever. I thought I could help."

"You, My Lady?"

"I have some skill with herbcraft," I replied.

"Please come in," she told me and led me inside the little house.

I turned to the soldiers. "I'll call if I need you."

They shifted uncomfortably but said nothing.

Within, the place was over warm and smelled of the animals who shared the home. The air felt sticky. From the back of the house, I heard a small cough. I followed the woman who led me to the back where three children lay on pallets. Each looked deathly pale. The smallest, a little girl, coughed miserably. At once I knew she had an infection in her chest.

"May I?" I asked, kneeling down beside the little girl.

Flora nodded.

"Well, now, little lass," I said, sitting beside the girl. She had hair the color of straw and wide blue eyes. Her brothers looked wide-eyed at me from their bed nearby. "Sounds like you swallowed a frog. Have you? Did your brothers slip a frog into your broth?" I asked her.

Despite themselves, all three children giggled.

"It hurts when I swallow," the little girl said.

"Me too," one of her brothers added.

I set my hand on her forehead. She was hot with fever. "Let me see inside that throat," I told her.

The girl opened her mouth wide. Inside, I saw red sores inside her mouth trailing down to her throat.

"May I?" I asked, pulling her blankets aside. "I want to see your feet."

She nodded.

As I expected, I saw her feet were covered with blisters, as were her hands.

"Hmm," I noised, nodding thoughtfully then shifted to look at the boys. "Now, the two of you," I told them, finding them in the same condition as their sister.

"Tell me, do you children mind your mother well?" I asked them.

They all nodded.

"If I give her something for you to drink, even though it tastes like sour stump water, will you drink it?"

They grimaced but nodded.

I turned to Flora. "Air the place out and change their bedding. Then I want you to give them each a draft," I said, opening the box I'd brought with me. I mixed several herbs, including lemon balm, peppermint, and other helpful ingredients, then handed it to her. "Brew the herbs into a draft and give it to them, each from their own cup, twice a day," I said. I then handed her an oil mixture. "This is for their hands and feet. Be sure you wash your hands with hot water between using it on each child. Send word to Cawdor if you see no improvement in two days."

"To Cawdor?" the little girl asked.

"This is the Lady of Moray," her mother informed her.

"Are you really?" the girl asked, her eyes going wide.

I nodded. "I heard the three of you were not feeling well. I came to see you."

The children smiled excitedly. "Really?" the little girl asked.

I smiled at her. "Now promise me you'll drink the draft? No complaints?"

"We'll do it, My Lady."

I smiled. "Very well," I said, then rose to go.

"Thank...thank you, Lady Gruoch," Flora told me.

I nodded to her then headed back outside. With a smile, James helped me back into the wagon.

"James MacNess, by the Great Mother, thank you for bringing our lady here," Flora told him.

My escort smiled. "She insisted."

I waved to Flora, and we set off once more. I was careful to clean my hands as Epona instructed me as we rode. The last thing I wanted was to spread an illness that seemed to have a mind of its own.

We rode then into the little village of Nairn. Since most people lived on nearby farms, Nairn was not much more than a marketplace and a few scattered houses. Many people, however, were gathered near the center well when we arrived. Gillacoemgain's soldiers, I noted, were met with suspicion.

I gazed out at the Moray Firth, the expansive body of water nearby. A sweet wind whipped off the dark blue water. The air felt warm and fresh. After a bit, James had collected many parents and elders. I went at once to meet with them, listening to them describe the same symptoms Flora's children were afflicted with. And once more, I dispensed the same medicines and advice. I could see in their eyes, that the people of Moray were both surprised and grateful. And finally, I felt like I was doing the Lady's work.

I was packing up my boxes when a woman in the crowd approached me.

"You're Boite's daughter," she said.

I smiled at the old woman. She was bent, white-haired, and far advanced in age. She reminded me of Andraste. "Yes, Mother," I told her.

The old woman eyed me curiously. "You're with child," she said, her eyes twinkling. "Looks like my knot magic worked."

"Knot magic?" I looked at her closely. She had an air of magic about her.

"In your wedding gown. It was me who sewed it for you. The magic is in the stitches," she said, but then added, "but of course you know about such things."

"I do. And, yes, I am with child."

The woman leaned against the center well and nodded thoughtfully. "I've seen you in the cauldron," she told me then.

"Have you?"

"You, but not you. I've seen the raven."

I stilled. I cast a glance at James and the soldiers. Busy with the villagers, they had not heard. "And what was the raven doing?"

"What the raven does so well. Let it loose," she said, "when the time comes." She gazed at my belly. "Twins."

I nodded, wondering how much more she knew.

She laughed. "Be well, daughter of Boite. Moray is

your home now. You are welcome amongst her people," she said then wandered off.

It was then that James gently took my arm. "My Lady of Moray, there is a gentleman here I'd like you to meet. An acquaintance of mine had come to market in search of a new horse. Perhaps you'd like to meet Douglas?"

I grinned. "Lead the way."

As I walked through the busy market, the people of Moray smiled and stopped to thank me. My heart filled with joy.

James then led me to a horse fair. Six horses were up for bid.

"Which is he?" I whispered to James.

"Black hair. Long beard."

I motioned to Standish who joined me.

"Do you carry any coin?"

At first, he looked surprised then he laughed. "Have your eye on something, Lady Gruoch?"

"In a way."

"I do."

"May I borrow it?"

Standish handed me his coin pouch. I went amongst the horses and inspected them all, settling on the best colt offered that day. There was no doubt Douglas had also noticed the horse, but he was angling for something cheap.

"You there," I said, calling to Douglas. "What do you think of this colt?"

Douglas, who'd been lost in thought, turned and looked at me. I realized then he was noticing me for the first time. The farmer next to him leaned into his ear and whispered something. I saw his eyes go wide.

"My Lady," he said awkwardly. "Finest beast amongst the bunch," he said then smiled, pleased I'd asked his opinion.

The horse trader eyed me skeptically, but catching sight of James, the expression on his face told me he suspected the ruse.

"I'll take him," I told the horse trader then turned to Douglas. "A bride token for a friend. He wishes to wed his neighbor's daughter. Do you think the horse is enough?"

Douglas stroked his beard. "Depends. How many daughters does the man have?"

I could see he still had not caught on to my game. The horse trader handed the colt's lead to me.

"Five," I replied.

"Oh yes, that and a few sheep or goats would do."

"A fair trade, you think?" I asked Douglas.

He nodded.

I motioned to James. "Master Douglas has agreed to the deal. Here you are, sir," I said, handing the lead to Douglas. "I'll have the sheep sent from Cawdor this afternoon. When can James expect your daughter?"

Douglas looked from James to me then to the colt and back to me again. He laughed out loud. "The Lady of

Moray has outwitted me, lads," he called to his friends who laughed good-naturedly. "Come for dinner tonight, lad," he told James. "We'll settle the matter then and you can tell me how you got the Mormaer's wife to bargain on your behalf."

"Thank you, Douglas," James said then bowed to me.

"I'll ride back with my men," I told him. "Why don't you head home and get your house ready for your bride."

James laughed. "Our first daughter will be named Gruoch, I promise you, Lady."

"Oh, please don't. Name her Emer for my mother."

James bowed.

I turned to Standish. "I'm ready. Mind if I ride with you?"

Chuckling, he shook his head. "I'm ready when you are."

With that, I mounted behind Standish then left the small village of Nairn, pleased that I had done the Lady's work.

CHAPTER FOURTEEN

The fever that swept through Moray took some work to defeat, but I worked tirelessly to stamp it out. I'd planted herb gardens in the small garden in the unused part of the castle near the chapel. As I suspected, the ground there was good. I could feel the otherworld close to me there, despite the presence of the chapel. As I worked, I felt eyes on me. When the herbs grew faster and larger than they should have, further proving my assumptions, I brewed medicines which I distributed to the people who came seeking my help. Word had spread through the countryside that the Lady of Moray was gifted in herbcraft. Soon, I found all manner of people at my door seeking help. It pleased me to busy myself helping the people of Moray as my little ones grew inside me.

I was hard at work one late summer morning, on my hands and knees amongst the basil and spearmint, when I heard boot steps along the stone walkway leading to the small garden. No doubt, it was time for lunch. Already the little babes inside me were fluttering about hungrily.

"Just a few more minutes," I said. "I'm half-bathed in soil," I added with a laugh, clapping the rich dirt off my hands. When I did so, I picked up the sharp scents of the herbs.

"Corbie?"

I turned to find Gillacoemgain standing there. He looked dirty and road-weary, his shoulders drooping from tire. He was staring at me, a confused look on his face.

Moving slowly, the burden of my belly already bothering me, I rose.

I'd been wearing a pair of Gillacoemgain's old breeches under my dress so I could kneel down on the soil. I wiped off the dirt then dropped the skirt of my lavender colored gown, suddenly aware of how sweaty and messy I was.

Gillacoemgain's eyes drifted to my stomach. Word, I realized then, had not yet reached the Mormaer's ears of my pregnancy.

"You're..." he whispered, looking closely at me. "Corbie?"

I smiled. I had told the lie to myself so many times, so many nights, that the children were his that when the moment came to tell him, I almost believed it. "I'm pregnant."

Gillacoemgain crossed the space between us quickly. He wrapped his arms around me and pressed his face into my neck. "Sweet wife. The north is quiet. My wife is with child. There is nothing more in this world a man could want."

He kissed me then, strongly and passionately, and I felt the love pour from him.

A moment later, he sighed heavily, and I felt his mood shift. "Artos," he said, nearly growling the name. "He met me at the gate to tell me you've spent the whole summer roaming the countryside and had been using the part of the castle I'd closed. He never said a word... just whipped me into a fury while he complained bitterly. I came here to..."

"To?"

"With anger in my heart," Gillacoemgain admitted.

"No one told me. Artos, in particular, though he knew I was working here. He has been a problem these many months. I didn't think it wise to let him speak on your behalf. I've taken over the public hearings. I didn't want him to speak in our name."

Gillacoemgain nodded. "So he complained, and rumored you were doing a poor job at it," he said then half-smiled at me, "which I doubted. Artos was part of my father's court. I kept him on in good faith."

"He does not treat the people of Moray fairly. His decisions and actions further promote the false…reputation you have."

Gillacoemgain frowned. "He'll be gone by nightfall."

I looked around the garden. "It's such a lovely space. I planted herbs here, medicines. There has been a sickness in Moray. The herbs…I used them to make tonics," I said then peered closely at Gillacoemgain. A pained look twisted his tired features. "Why did you close this side of the castle? They did tell me your brother once resided here."

Gillacoemgain gently wiped dirt off my cheek. "That chamber," he said, pointing to a room above the garden, "is where my sister was murdered."

"Murdered?" I gasped, looking up. "How?"

Gillacoemgain took my hand and led me to a bench nearby. He looked up at the window, and I could see the deep sorrow in his face. Something bad had happened, something he would rather not remember. But he was tired, and when we are in such a state, the stuff inside us that steels us to sorrow weakens.

"The story that everyone knows is that my sister fell in her chamber, hit her head, and died. But I…I know the truth of the matter. Findelach was my elder brother, and all our lives he was cruel to both my sister and me. He was a rough child, and my father boasted that one day he would be a great warrior. He was. But he was also a cruel man. When he went to Inverness to be with his wife and child, I thought my sister, Crearwy, and I had escaped him. I kept her here with me, kept her safe until a husband could be found for her. I long suspected my brother had... mistreated our sister, but she would never say so. But it was there, in that chamber, when I saw the truth for myself. My poor, sweet sister. He had...he used her as a brother should not use his sister...and beat her besides. I found her half dead. Findelach escaped, and my sister died in my arms. For that reason, I followed my brother to the ends of Moray and snuffed out his life. You must swear to me, Corbie, not to tell the truth of this. Swear it. But I wanted you to know. You might carry the child of a man who killed his own brother, but I did it for a good reason."

I stared up at the closed casement. Was the world full of cruel men? Did we walk amongst vicious people who hid behind false smiles? Behind closed doors, how many women suffered at the hands of men who were supposed to care for them? My heart broke for Crearwy, the sister-in-law I would never know, and for my husband who'd borne the secret. "I swear to keep your secret like it was my own," I said, lacing my fingers between his. "I'll move the garden," I told him.

He shook his head. "Crearwy would have loved it. Grow your herbs here so her spirit can enjoy them."

Gillacoemgain set his hands on my stomach. "So big already?"

"In Nairn, a woman told me I carried twins."

Gillacoemgain laughed. "So you shall carry my sun and my moon," he said then turned serious. "Why did you go out? You know I had asked you not to."

"The children of Moray…there was an illness. I went out to ensure that the next generation of people in this land were healthy and strong. I went out to save lives," I said, realizing then the complex nature of the Mother Goddess: she was both a life-bringer and a destroyer. Despite the fact that it was the dark goddesses who seemed to rule over my fate, it was the Great Mother who'd coached my hands all these months. As I grew ripe with life, I practiced her earthy magic.

Gillacoemgain nodded then sighed heavily, as if he had no good retort for my answer. "I'm weary, wife. And you're as dirty as I am. Come, let's have your maid draw us a bath."

I laughed. I had, in fact, missed Gillacoemgain's touch. More often than I cared to admit, his taste and the feel of his body came to my mind. And while Banquo lingered forever around the edges of my heart, Gillacoemgain had been foremost in my thoughts the past few months.

"After you," I said, smiling up at him.

"You smell like mint," he told me, planting a kiss on my cheek.

"You smell like horses."

He laughed. "Come then, my wife, and let me see that belly," he said, leading me away.

I cast one look back at the garden as we left, and this time, I saw the ethereal figure of a girl with long black hair standing amongst the herbs, smiling at me.

CHAPTER FIFTEEN

*G*illacoemgain spent most of the next two days in bed, barely waking to eat something. I didn't know what he had seen or what difficulties he'd faced, but the weight of it on him was obvious. I crept quietly in and out of our chamber where he dozed, bringing him meals and snuggling in beside him. On the morning of the third day, however, when I arrived with his morning meal, I found him awake and getting dressed.

"I was just about to come looking for you. I wanted to check on my birds. Come with me?"

I set the tray on a table. "Are you hungry? I brought all your favorite—" I began, but Gillacoemgain crossed the room and silenced me with a kiss.

The depth of his passion took my breath away. For the first time, I sensed joy in him. Since we'd first met,

Gillacoemgain had been worried by the state of affairs in Moray. Now, with that burden lifted from him, I saw a spark of his true self.

When he finally let me go, I laughed. "Of course. Let's go," I said.

Gillacoemgain and I headed outside, crossing the yard to the stables where his falcons were kept.

"My Lord?" Standish said, falling into step with us.

"How are my birds?" Gillacoemgain asked.

"We've been keeping them exercised. I put one of the lads in charge of them. He has a way with animals and has taken good care of them. I think he's back there now."

Gillacoemgain nodded.

"My Lady," Standish added, smiling at me. "The little one has your cheeks looking rosy as apples today."

Gillacoemgain smiled and set his hand on my stomach. "What do you think, Standish? Boy or girl?"

"Or both, from the looks of her," Standish said.

"Wouldn't that be a blessing?" Gillacoemgain said, putting his arm around me and pulling me close.

"That dog of yours is out here somewhere, Lady. I just saw her run past, nose to the ground, hot on the trail of something."

I nodded. Gillacoemgain patted the man on the shoulder, and we headed toward the mews where the falcons were housed. A few moments later, I heard Thora bark happily. We turned the corner to find Thora waiting patiently while a young boy held a small bit of bread for her.

"Down," the boy told her.

Thora lay on the ground and looked up at the boy expectantly.

I laughed out loud.

At the sound of my voice, Thora turned and offered me a muffled bark.

The boy also looked at me. It was the same lad I'd seen with Thora from time to time. This was, however, the first time I'd seen him up close. He was a lovely child with smooth skin, curly brown hair, and sparkling green eyes. I had seen eyes like that once before...on Sid. I also noticed the shimmering glow of the otherworld around him. A half fey thing, perhaps?

"M'Lord, M'Lady!" he said happily, tossing the bread to Thora.

"So you're the one who has kept Thora busy," I said.

The boy nodded. "Yes, M'Lady. She's a clever one."

Gillacoemgain tousled his hair. "How are my falcons? I hear you've been keeping care of them."

"Yes, M'Lord. They are doing well. I've been taking them out every day, letting them get their exercise."

"What's your name?" I asked, still eyeing the boy who seemed to avoid eye contact with me.

"Eochaid, M'Lady."

"Well, let's have a go then," Gillacoemgain said. He

slipped on a long, heavy leather glove then opened the door to the mew, coaxing one of the falcons to him.

Thora, I noticed, perked up.

"I hope you don't mind, Lady Gruoch, but I've been running your bonnie lass here with the birds. She'd good at flushing pheasants," Eochaid told me.

"Is she now?" I said, smiling down at Thora who looked like she'd been caught red-handed. "And, no doubt, in exchange for some of the winnings."

Eochaid laughed. "Rabbits, when she can find them."

I shook my head. "Naughty thing," I said to her, but Thora just wagged her tail.

Gillacoemgain, Eochaid, and I then headed out into the field nearby, Thora following along beside me. The summer grass had grown tall. Purple asters, oxeye daisies, and buttercups painted the field with color.

As we walked, Gillacoemgain spoke in soft tones to the bird resting on his arm. The bird eyed him closely, clearly familiar with the sound of his master's voice. Without fear of getting bit, Gillacoemgain petted the bird's head, stroking his soft feathers.

"Well now, Thora. Seems all my girls have been busy running outside the castle walls in my absence. Let's see if you've been as successful as your lady," Gillacoemgain told my dog when we came to a thick patch of grass.

Eochaid whistled and directed Thora toward the field.

She zipped into the grass. The only thing you could

see was the tip of her tail as she moved quickly through the field. We waited awhile then heard Thora's muffled bark.

"She's got them. Be ready," Eochaid told Gillacoemgain.

A moment later, we heard the sound of wings as startled pheasants rose out of the grass.

Thora barked loudly.

Gillacoemgain directed the bird and sent her on her way. The falcon sped away quickly, diving with her sharp talons toward the birds. The intense sound of her wings caught me off guard, and the raven within me seemed to spark to life. It was all I could do to keep my spirit inside me. A moment later, the falcon returned, a pheasant in her claws.

She flew back to Gillacoemgain.

"Well done," he told her. "That one is yours," he added, sending her off to a nearby tree so she could enjoy the spoils of her work.

Thora came trotting back, looking at Eochaid expectantly. From his pocket, the boy pulled out a bit of dried beef that he tossed to her.

We hunted most of the morning, roaming through the fields, soaking in the summer sun. I kept my eyes on the ground while Gillacoemgain and the boy worked. I'd stuffed many herbs and roots into my pockets. My hands were covered in soil and the summer sun had me sweating, but I felt truly at ease.

I had just helped myself to a handful of wild-growing raspberries when I heard Gillacoemgain and the boy laughing. I gazed back at them. Gillacoemgain was clapping the boy gently on the back in congratulations when the falcon returned with a rabbit. It was such a sweet scene. I set my hand on my stomach. Inside, two babes were growing. Perhaps they were not Gillacoemgain's blood, but they were mine, and it was clear to me that Gillacoemgain was going to be a loving father.

I smiled happily and closed my eyes, feeling the warm summer sun shining down on my dark hair. The sweet taste of raspberries filled my mouth, the sound of a child's laughter on the wind. Could there ever have been a more perfect moment? I sighed contentedly, feeling the little ones within me stir. They were moving more and more each day, especially when I ate something they loved. Taking out a handkerchief, I picked a few more berries then rejoined Gillacoemgain and Eochaid.

As I did so, I heard the roll of thunder in the far distance.

"A storm is coming," Gillacoemgain said, pointing to dark clouds on the horizon. In the distance, the sweet blue of the summer's sky faded into a thick bank of clouds. "Let's head back."

"Thora," I called, but the dog was still off looking for trouble.

"Fey thing, your bonnie lass," Eochaid said. "Half the time I think she slips between the worlds. One minute she's nowhere in sight, the next she's right beside you," he told me.

I looked down at the child. He had a mischievous look on his face. "You know, I've heard the same thing said about little boys...wild, fey things, such as they are."

Eochaid winked at me. "I'm sure M'Lady knows of such things much better than me."

"Indeed?"

Eochaid smiled.

I handed my handkerchief full of raspberries to the boy. "Sweets for the sweet," I told him.

"Thank you, M'Lady," he said, grinning happily at my harvest.

"And for you," I told Gillacoemgain, handing him the only two wild strawberries I'd found that morning.

He shook his head. "You," he told me, "one for each of my little ones."

I laughed then ate. It had taken all my willpower to save them in the first place.

Thunder rolled again as we returned to the castle. I could smell the rain in the breeze now, and the air was charged with the power of the storm. We were just putting the falcon back in her cage when Thora appeared.

"Have fun?" I asked her.

She wagged her tail in reply.

"Thank you, Eochaid," Gillacoemgain told the boy. "How long have you been at Cawdor?"

"Since spring. I came around the same time Lady Gruoch arrived."

Gillacoemgain nodded. "I see you've taken good care of my birds. I'll see to it Standish knows."

"Thank you, M'Lord," Eochaid said, and when he smiled, I swore I saw Sid in his face once more. It was the fey glow.

I nodded to the boy and waved at Thora to follow.

As we passed through the yard, I saw that everyone was readying for the storm. The geese were herded into their pens, horses being stabled.

"Why don't you go in? I can check on Kelpie," Gillacoemgain told me, then kissed me on the forehead.

Thora and I headed inside as the first crack of lightning struck not too far away.

"So, where have you been going?" I asked Thora who tilted her head at me. "Back at Ynes Verleath or off playing with Sid?"

Thora barked.

"Off with Sid and Nadia then?"

Thora wagged her tail.

"Fey thing indeed," I said. I headed back up to the chamber I shared with Gillacoemgain. I opened the casement to get a good look at the storm headed our way. As I did, I spotted Eochaid crossing the yard, a gaggle of kittens following along behind him as he lured them into shelter with a saucer of milk. How many times had the child been nearby when I needed help? Who was that wee lad? This time, I shifted my focus and looked with my raven's eyes. When I did, I couldn't help but notice the glimmer of shimmering golden light, a tiny glimmering ball, zipping around him everywhere he went.

"Nadia?"

Lightning clapped once more, capturing my attention. I looked off in the distance. On the horizon, threads of light shot across the sky.

When my eyes drifted back, however, I saw the golden light that had been shimmering all around Eochaid flying toward me. I looked hard, trying to part the veil between us, to really see. When I did, I discovered it was not Nadia who kept the boy company but a male fairy.

He was there and gone in just a blink of an eye, and in that single second, I realized that the little fairy man had bowed to me. In a flash, the fairy man returned to the boy who was now picking up all the kittens in an effort to get them inside just as the first drops of rain fell. He looked to be holding ten puffy balls. I laughed out loud.

At that, Eochaid looked up, smiled at me, and then headed within. Fey, indeed.

CHAPTER SIXTEEN

hat night, the thunder boomed loudly, lightning streaking across the sky. I lay watching flashes of light through the cracks in the closed window casement.

"Can't sleep?" Gillacoemgain asked, his hand sliding up my side, resting on my stomach.

I shook my head then sighed. "No. It's too hot and too loud. The air is alive with too much magic."

"I feel it as well," Gillacoemgain said. "My mother taught me to be mindful of the old things, the old ways. My father adopted the appearance of worship of the White Christ, but my mother's lessons stayed with me. I...I do feel the otherworld around us. When I am alone in the woods, I would swear I can feel Cernunnos' presence."

In the darkness, I smiled. "He is the lord of the forest

and the hunt. It is only natural that you, who love such things, feel kinship toward him."

Gillacoemgain sighed. "I've never had time to spend thinking about such things," he said, then stroked the back of my arm. The sensation shot chills up and down my body.

"Perhaps, now that all is quiet…"

"Yes," Gillacoemgain said, pushing my hair away so he could kiss my neck. "I will have time now, for that, for my wife, for my little ones."

I rolled over and looked at him in the darkness. One candle lit in our chamber, but the lightning outside flashed endlessly, illuminating his face. How handsome he was, his rugged chin and alluring eyes.

Gillacoemgain smiled at me, his left cheek taking on a dimple, then leaned in and kissed me. His mouth was warm and tasted of the honeyed herb tonic he'd drunk after dinner. I caught his sweet scent, that woodsy smell mixed with the lavender.

"I know you are heavy with child. If I am careful… would you?"

I nodded. "Yes," I breathed. In that moment, more than anything, I wanted to feel him. Gillacoemgain of Moray. Beyond all chance, my heart had turned to him.

Moving carefully, he pulled off my nightdress then discarded his own clothes onto the floor. He lay his cheek on my bare stomach, kissing my swollen belly.

"I'm so proud of you," he whispered then, his hands

dancing toward my breasts. "I'm so proud you are my wife," he said, kissing my neck, his mouth drifting down to my breasts, his hand moving between my legs.

I gasped when he touched me, my hands feeling for him in the darkness.

"As I am of you," I whispered in reply before a moan escaped my lips.

Gillacoemgain said no more then, as his mouth trailed down my body to my secret parts where he gave me pleasure like I'd never known before in all my life. And I, in turn, sought to please the man whom I had grown to love.

*O*nce the storm arrived, it didn't leave for days. The yard became a muddy mess as rain poured down relentlessly. The stream running near Cawdor, which poured into the River Nairn, started to break its banks. Gillacoemgain rode out with Fergus, Standish, and a few others to investigate the farms that sat close to the water.

Since I dared not brave the weather, I went instead to check on my garden which had also turned into a watery mess. The water in the small castle courtyard pooled amongst the stones. It rained too fast for it to run off properly. My herbs were drowning. I spent the morning digging drains so the water would wash away. By midday, I was, despite the shelter from castle awnings, wet and tired.

But I was also unreasonably curious. Since the day I had seen her shade, I wondered about Crearwy, Gillacoemgain's sister. Knowing he was away, I left my work and crept up the back hallways to the unused section of the castle.

It was clear that this section of Cawdor had once been part of the regular household. Candles still sat in the tapers, tapestries adorned the walls. I lit a candle and went exploring.

The space was full of cobwebs and covered in dust. The chambers still had chairs and tables, dishes and goblets, beds, but no one had been there in years. I pushed open a chamber to see the bed was still made but covered in inches of dust. I moved down the hall to the room Gillacoemgain had mentioned. All the while, my raven eyes peered around for the shade. I didn't know why I wanted to see her, but something drove me.

I entered a shuttered hallway. No light save the small candle I held illuminated the space. I was struck at once by the feeling of magic. My skin rose in goosebumps as I moved down the hall. I couldn't see the chamber at the other end, but I knew I was somewhere thin. I walked past a window when a sharp breeze blew in, snuffing out my candle.

I steeled the fear that wanted to rise up inside me and

moved ahead, reaching in the darkness for the door handle.

My fingers brushed against the cold metal handle. Pulling the chamber door open, I stepped into a dark space.

It took my eyes a moment to adjust.

I had expected to find a simple bedchamber, but as my eyes settled in, what I found was something quite different. I was standing just outside my bedchamber in Ynes Verleath. At once, the smell of wisteria assailed my nose. I closed my eyes and inhaled deeply, taking in the sweet scent. Quite by accident, I had walked between the worlds.

I walked out to the terrace where Andraste stood stirring the cauldron. Nimue dropped sprigs of herbs into the pot.

"By the pricking of my thumb, a certain sister this way comes," Andraste said, looking up at me.

"How now, Andraste? Nimue? Why have you called me here?"

Nimue smiled at me, but I saw she wore a sad expression behind her smile. She dropped a feather into the cauldron.

"Be bloody, bold, and resolute," Andraste said. "All will burn. Make your heart ready, Cerridwen."

"And more," Nimue said.

"Hover through the fog, the snow, the filthy air. There to meet with Macbeth," Andraste intoned.

"Macbeth?"

"Anon," Andraste said, waving me away.

"Anon," Nimue told me with a broken smile.

A moment later, I felt a small hand in mine.

"M'Lady?" I heard someone call. "M'Lady?"

I recognized the youthful voice belonging to the lad, Eochaid.

"Eochaid?"

"They're searching the castle for you," he told me then. "I...I found...you know how. He...we knew where you were. Can I help you out of here, Lady? I don't think Lord Gillacoemgain will be pleased to find you here."

I was lying on the floor. From the dim light of Eochaid's lantern, I could see I was in a bedchamber in the closed section of the castle. I looked all around. I spotted a spindle, gowns hanging in a wardrobe, and other women's things. And on the floor nearby, I spotted a large, dark stain on the flagstones.

"Yes," I whispered. "Please."

Eochaid helped me up then led me to a tapestry on the other side of the room. Moving the musty tapestry aside, he led me down a set of winding stairs. The dust was thick there. Clearly, the space had not been used in years.

"It's not far," Eochaid reassured me. "Just this way."

A moment later, I smelled the cool, rain-soaked air. Eochaid and I emerged in a passageway not far from the chapel. The boy quickly led me to a door at the back of the chapel then inside.

"Stay here," he told me. "Tell them you came inside to shelter from the rain and fell asleep. I'll find you."

Still disoriented from my walk to the otherworld, I nodded. Was it night already or had the sky simply grown dark from the rain?

I sat down on one of the pews inside the chapel.

"She's here," I heard Eochaid call then. "Lord Gillacoemgain, she's here."

With Eochaid's lantern beside me, I sat waiting in the dark chapel.

"Macbeth?" I whispered to the darkness.

There was no reply.

"Gruoch?" I heard Gillacoemgain call, his voice full of worry. "Gruoch?"

"I'm here," I said, standing. My knees were shaking.

Gillacoemgain entered the back of the chapel then rushed across the room quickly, pulling me into an embrace. "Corbie, where have you been? No one could find you."

"I…" I began, passing a look to the boy who stood by the chapel door, "I was working in the garden when the rain started falling hard. I came into the chapel to wait out the downpour. I guess I must have fallen asleep."

Gillacoemgain stared at me, and I saw the look of fear and worry leave his face. He laughed out loud.

"Lord Gillacoemgain?" I heard Standish call.

"She's here. She's fine."

Shaking his head, Gillacoemgain offered me his hand then led me out of the chapel. Eochaid, who was staying out of the way, smiled at me, nodded, and then ran off.

"Should have known, a pregnant woman can fall asleep anywhere," Gillacoemgain said, shaking his head.

Understanding, Standish laughed. "You gave us a scare, Lady. Here we thought maybe Thorfinn had come and abducted you."

"No, I..." I began, shaking my head. "I'm very sorry. I just fell asleep."

Gillacoemgain kissed me on the forehead. "Let's get my Lady to bed."

Slowly coming back to myself, I realized then that Gillacoemgain was soaked. "You're wet from head to toe."

He nodded. "It's bad out there. Lots of livestock lost, damaged crops. Hopefully, the rains end soon."

I nodded, part of my mind rushing quickly down the list of farms along the stream, but more of me was focused on a single name: *Macbeth*.

CHAPTER SEVENTEEN

hough many in Moray wanted to paint Gillacoemgain as a ruthless warlord, each day he rode out to check on cattle, fortify levees, and move his people to higher ground as the floodwaters rolled in. Some warlord. After a few weeks, however, the waters subsided, and Moray returned to a peaceful calm. The harvest season was soon upon us, and the air grew cold, the leaves turning hues of sunset orange, deep red, and vibrant yellow. Despite Andraste's ominous words, the north, at least, seemed to be at peace. Word came that Malcolm was at odds once more with King Cnut of England and was amassing forces to go march south once more. And Macbeth, Gillacoemgain's nephew, was at King Malcolm's side, a virtual prisoner. I had nothing to do with Macbeth. What in the world was Andraste speaking of?

"Will Malcolm call on Moray for support?" I asked Gillacoemgain one night as we rested in front of the fire in the main hall.

"He may," Gillacoemgain said, sipping his hot apple cider, which I'd spiced with herbs.

Not only was my husband not a murdering warlord, he was neither a drunkard nor a lecher. Occasionally he took a glass of wine, but only occasionally. I never saw his eyes on another woman. He was a quiet, peaceful man. When he wasn't busy helping the people of Moray, he hunted, fished, and trained his birds, always returning with a woodland flower or wild herb for me. In the evenings, we rested together, Gillacoemgain watching my growing belly with great interest.

"I can see your stomach moving," he said, setting his hands on my stomach. "Does it hurt?"

I shook my head. "I'm weary, and feel like I can't breathe at times, but it doesn't hurt."

"Any ideas for names?" he asked.

I shook my head. I had, in truth, tried to come up with something. But nothing felt just right.

"If one is a boy, perhaps we should name him Boite for your father. Boite...I will never forget him, marching into my father's hall in Inverness with his men around him. He was like a giant with his long black hair and an enormous sword dangling from his belt. I remember my father falling to his knee before him. I had never seen my father bow to anyone. I'll never forget it."

"I spent little time with him, but I adored him," I said, remembering the last time I saw my father in Madelaine's hall. I had truly loved him.

"Boite, then?"

I sent my hand on my stomach, lacing my fingers with Gillacoemgain's. "No. That doesn't feel right."

Gillacoemgain kissed the top of my head. "We'll think of something."

Despite the heavy summer rains, with autumn came the harvest. Cawdor's stores were filled to capacity with grains and roots. I moped around for what felt like days, dreaming of the wild strawberries I'd found in the field that summer. Why hadn't I thought to save it and try to grow my own plants in my garden?

Early one morning, as I was crossing the square to harvest the last of my plants, I met with Eochaid.

"Lady Gruoch," he called, rushing toward me, carrying a large bucket.

I stopped and waited for him. Since that episode during the flood, the boy and I had always kept an eye out for one another. He was part fey, just as Sid was, and he knew what I was. He might have called me "M'Lady," but I knew he saw Cerridwen. I hadn't tried to see the little fairy man again, but I knew he was there. I could feel him.

"Eochaid. Good morning, lad. What do you have there?"

The boy handed me the wooden bucket. Inside, I

found a heap of blackberries, raspberries, and straw-berries.

I gasped. "How?"

Eochaid smiled at me, that enticing fey glamor emanating from him. "Easy to find, if you know where to look…and if you have a little help."

I bent over and kissed the boy on the forehead. "Thank you, Eochaid. Why don't you come into the castle to work? It will turn cold soon. I'll ask Gillacoemgain to take you on as a page."

Eochaid shook his head. "I can't leave his Lordship's birds. They'd miss me too much. Don't worry about me, Lady Gruoch. I can find my way around."

I set the bucket down and knelt to look the boy in the eye. It should have been an easy movement, but the weight of the babies had me off kilter. Laughing, Eochaid reached out to steady me.

"You don't have to say a thing," he told me then.

"No, I don't. But I want to make sure you know that you always have a place in my household. If you need anything, ask me. If anyone mistreats you, tell me. What can I do for you? Would you want to apprentice under the master of horse? Look after Kelpie too?"

He tipped his head as if he were thinking it over. "May I still keep watch on the falcons?"

"Of course."

"Then I would."

"I'll see to it then."

Eochaid smiled. "Thank you, M'Lady. And enjoy the berries. Hope you don't mind I had a couple," he said, showing me the blueberry stains on his hands.

I laughed. "Not at all."

With a nod, he ran off then, back toward the stables.

As I watched him go, I smiled. Perhaps I would have two boys. What a pair of monsters they would be. But even as the thought crossed my mind, a flicker of memory sprang up, the feel of Duncan's hands on me, the smell of the wet mud.

I closed my eyes and forced the image away. I would take my vengeance on him. One day he would pay for what he'd done to me. But now, I was in no condition to do anything except carry his seed, all the while telling myself it was Gillacoemgain's.

Sighing, I picked up the berries and headed back to my garden. Most of my herbs had gone to seed. I wanted to gather the last of them before it was too late, and before I was too big to do so. I sat a little while in the garden, gathering bunches of herbs, my eyes drifting up toward Crearwy's chamber.

Even though it was just for a moment, I had seen the blood stain on the floor. Even if I'd doubted Gillacoemgain's story, the proof was in how Crearwy's room had been left, her clothes and belongings sitting right where she'd left them. I sighed. And there, in that dark space, I'd found my way back to Ynes Verleath.

Andraste had said, *Hover through the fog, the snow, the*

filthy air. There to meet with Macbeth. But typical of Andraste, she'd riddled, always waiting for time to solve the mysteries she set before me.

I cast a glance once more up at Crearwy's chamber. This time, I spotted light and movement through the slats in the door that led to the terrace overlooking the garden. I watched a moment, hoping I wasn't seeing fairy globes, when once more I saw golden light shimmer behind the door. Candlelight? Who was in the chamber?

I stashed the herbs in my bucket and rose slowly, then headed up the stairs toward the terrace. It was so silent on this end of the castle. I could just make out the sound of Standish's voice coming from the yard. Otherwise, there was only the wind. The air smelled of wood smoke and venison. That morning, they'd stoked the great fire high in order to roast the spoils of Gillacoemgain's early morning hunt. He'd gone out at dawn, returning with a doe. But the fire had another purpose. The nights were becoming very cold. The scent of not-far-off snow filled the air. Carrying a candle with me, I walked down the dark hallway once more to the interior chamber door.

I heard movement inside the room and could see the glow of a candle.

"Not Ynes Verleath," I whispered, pushing power behind my words. I did not want to fall into the otherworld again.

I set my hand on the handle and quietly opened the door.

Inside, I found someone sitting on the floor. There was a strange scratching sound.

The light of my candle caught his attention. From his position on the floor, Gillacoemgain looked up at me. I realized then what was happening. By the dim light of a single candle, he'd been working with a brush and bucket of water scrubbing the stain on the floor. The old blood, too stubborn to lift off, had marred his hands with an odd orange color.

"Out, damned spot," he said, looking hopelessly from the spot on the floor to me. "No matter what I do, I cannot make it go away. The blood won't wash away, from my mind, my heart, or this damned floor," he whispered. "Sometimes, I cannot bear the memories." I realized then his cheeks were wet with tears.

I knelt down beside him and wrapped my arms around him.

He stuffed his head into the crook of my neck and wept. "How could he?" he moaned.

I shook my head. "This world is full of evil men. Some men may seek to hide their foul deeds, but such wickedness will rise no matter how they try to hide it. Such as it was for your brother. Such as it will one day be for Malcolm. And for so many others who earn their bloody fates."

"My sister," Gillacoemgain said, looking down at the

spot on the floor. He shook his head. "Just a wee slip of a girl, about the same age as you. She will never love, nor be a mother. Her candle was snuffed out before she lived."

"Then we shall live for her. We will live and love and have many children. Through you, she will carry on."

Gillacoemgain looked around the room. "I should get rid of all these things."

"No. Let's see if we have a daughter. If we do, let her enjoy those things your sister held dear."

Gillacoemgain looked down at his hands, realizing then they were stained. "I'm sorry," he said.

I shook my head then reached out and wiped the tears off his face. "We all carry secret hurts inside us."

Gillacoemgain rose. "Let's go back. I need to wash…"

I nodded, rising slowly, Gillacoemgain reaching out to steady me, then lifted my bucket of berries. "Come inside. I'll bake you something sweet, and we'll try to forget our sorrows."

"Where did you find those?" Gillacoemgain asked.

"Eochaid," I said, walking back toward the door, beckoning Gillacoemgain to follow me. I knew I had to get him out of there, thinking of something else, away from the blood scene. "And to think, I've been craving strawberries all week."

Gillacoemgain smiled softly. "They are roasting the deer. I wanted you to eat well tonight. And now, a dessert too," he said, looking at the bucket and smiling.

"I wonder where he found them." Gillacoemgain shook his head in amazement. "I like that boy."

"As do I," I replied, walking beside my husband, leading him through the darkness back toward the light.

When we came to the garden once more, Gillacoemgain stopped and looked at what was left of my herbs. "Finished for the season."

I nodded. "Yes, I've just gathered the last of them to dry."

He gazed up once more at the chamber, sighed heavily, and then kissed the top of my head. "Love of my life," he whispered.

I looked up at him. For so long I had thought of Banquo as my soul's true love. But what if that love I'd felt for Banquo was just an echo of the past, of a life already lived by Boudicca and Prasutagus? What if that love had just been a youthful passion? When I looked at Gillacoemgain, I felt a deep well of gratitude, comradery, and love for the man gazing down at me.

"I love you," I told him.

He leaned down and planted a soft kiss on my lips.

"I'll meet you inside," he said, motioning that he was going to go to the stables.

I nodded and headed toward the kitchens. This time, I would remember to set berry seeds aside for planting next year but not before preparing Gillacoemgain, and Eochaid, the best tarts I'd ever made.

CHAPTER EIGHTEEN

*T*hat night, the entire household feasted on Gillacoemgain's deer and blueberry bread. I found Thora lying under Eochaid's feet at the servants' end of the table when I came to the boy with a tart wrapped in cloth.

"For later," I told him, slipping him the pastry.

"Many thanks, M'Lady," he said with a smile.

"The thanks go to you," I said then added, "and your friend. Does he have a name?"

Eochaid tipped his head as if to listen, like I'd seen Sid do so many times. The gesture seemed like a mirror of my old friend. "He says I can tell. He's named Eitri."

"Then many thanks to my good neighbor as well."

Eochaid smiled.

"And you, little lady, where have you been? Too busy hunting rabbits to check on your mistress?"

Thora rolled on her back to reveal a very full stomach. She wagged her tail, her tongue hanging out of the corner of her mouth. "Silly girl," I told her. "Just stay out of trouble."

After the meal was finished and the fire had died down, Gillacoemgain and I worked slowly upstairs to our chamber on the highest floor in the castle. After having to stop three times so I could catch my breath, Gillacoemgain shook his head.

"No more of this. Tomorrow, I'll have a bedchamber on the first floor prepared for you. It's too dangerous for you to climb so many steps. It may cause your water to break early."

I didn't disagree. The stairs had become too cumbersome, but I played with Gillacoemgain all the same, digging for his smile. "Admit it, I've grown so large I'm taking up too much of your bed. You just want more room."

Gillacoemgain laughed. "You certainly take up too much of my blankets. I woke with a frozen backside this morning."

"Well then, you need to snuggle in closer."

Once we were upstairs, my husband helped me lower myself into bed then tucked me in before crawling into the bed beside me. He wrapped his arms around me and held me tight. "What do you suppose they are, boys or girls?" he asked, putting his hands on my stomach. The little ones within my belly rolled. We could feel their kicks.

"Or one of each?"

Gillacoemgain kissed my shoulder. "Little raven," he whispered.

He was silent for a while thereafter and soon I heard his heavy breathing. He'd already drifted off to sleep.

Rest, for me, however, didn't come easy. No wonder poor Gillacoemgain had lost his blankets. I rolled most of the night, unable to find a comfortable position. It felt like half the night had passed when I heard scratching on the door.

I rose to find Thora outside.

"The boy kicked you out?" I asked her.

She wagged her tail then came inside, moving directly toward a spot in front of the fire.

"Good idea," I said then went to sit in a chair before the flames. I picked up the embroidery frame I'd been, albeit half-heartedly, working on, but felt too sleepy and too bored to bother. My eyelids drooped, but still, I didn't sleep. It must have been late in the evening when I saw movement in the room. At first I thought it was Thora moving around, but then I realized she was still at my feet. Out of the corner of my eye, a shape materialized.

"You're huge," a woman told me.

I recognized the sound of her voice at once. Sid. "What do you expect? I plan on bearing giants." I looked at her. She'd come by casting. She was a mere shadow of herself.

Thora lifted her head and wagged her tail.

Sid grinned. "So, how are you?"

"As well as can be expected."

"That bad? Come with me. We'll go visit the summer country and dance with the fey."

"And leave this swollen body behind? I don't think it advisable."

Sid laughed. "Where is the Mormaer?"

"Asleep," I said, motioning to the bed.

Sid went then to the bedside and looked down at him. How odd it was to see her, and see through her, all at once.

"You've always had good luck with men. He's rather a beast, isn't he? How is he...you know," she said, then motioned as if she were planning to lift the blankets and have a look.

"Sid!"

She laughed, her pleasant laughter tinkling like a bell.

Gillacoemgain sighed then rolled over.

"He is a man, all in all, but I've grown to love him," I told her.

"And what of your druid?"

Her abrupt question struck at my very core. "I've closed my heart to him."

"Liar."

"He's lost to me. It's best to forget him."

"I've seen him. He pines for you."

"You've seen him?"

"In the moonlight, amongst the rings, he weeps for the love he lost."

Banquo. "Comfort him," I told her.

"He has a wife for that."

"Yes, I know."

"But still, his heart longs for you."

"Why are you tormenting me with this?"

"Because I don't want you to forget."

"Forget what?"

"Who you really are," she said. "Who you really love."

"My love is in ashes."

Sid shook her head. "Malcolm, Epona, even that old hag, Andraste…they all play games. In your heart, you know to whom and to what life you really belong."

I looked at her, realizing in that moment what *she* needed from *me*. "I haven't forgotten you," I whispered. Like Banquo, Sid also held a special place in my heart, but it was a place I didn't quite understand. "I miss you. And I love you."

A look of relief crossed Sid's face. It was what she had longed to hear. A second later, however, she smothered the expression. "Of course you do. By the by, I come with a message."

"From whom?"

"Epona. She told me to ensure you remembered your promise. What did you promise her?"

"To come to the coven to deliver my children."

Sid looked thoughtful. "She seems dreadfully upset about the whole thing and worries excessively about you."

"Odd."

"Yes. These are odd times."

"Indeed?"

"Change is in the air. Will you be coming soon?"

I nodded. "I need to convince the Mormaer."

Sid looked back at him. "I can see how you could love a face like that," she said then sighed. Her casting weakened. "I must go."

"Begone then, spirit. Bother me no more," I said in jest.

We giggled.

Sid lifted a hand in farewell and then disappeared.

I was left staring into the flames, strange visions trying to take shape in my mind.

"Not tonight," I whispered to the darkness, to the Goddess, to the raven…to whoever wanted me to see what was to come. "Not tonight," I said, closing my eyes, my hands resting on my swollen belly.

Soon, someone whispered in reply, but I was too tired to understand if the voice had come from the other world or within me.

CHAPTER NINETEEN

"How will this do, Lady Gruoch?" Rhona, one of the household maids, asked me the next day as we stood in my new chamber. The household had been working hard all morning getting a room ready for me. They'd been at it even before I woke that morning, Gillacoemgain seeing to it that I had somewhere safe to rest during the day if I wanted.

The chamber was smaller than the one I shared with Gillacoemgain, but the bed was made with fresh straw and clean linens. The room had a good view of the comings and goings in the ward just outside, and a fireplace kept the space warm. Ute would have a small chamber just outside.

"It's perfect, Rhona, thank you."

"I'll move all your dresses down from your chamber," Ute told me, curtseying before she departed.

Thora tromped all around the bed.

"Well, is it comfortable?" I asked her.

She lay down at the foot of the bed and looked at me, tilting her head to the side.

I chuckled then went to the window, pushing open the casement. The temperature had dipped low and it had frosted overnight. The morning sun was burning away the last of the silver coating the grass. The air smelled of snow.

As I looked below, a messenger rode into Cawdor. It was not an unusual sight, but the rider's dress and horse caught my immediate attention. The horse, I noticed, had been worked into a lather. The rider, who wore a rich blue velvet doublet, look harried. One of the pages ran into the castle, presumably to get Gillacoemgain.

A few minutes later, Gillacoemgain crossed the ward and met the rider who handed him a paper. Standish came from the stables and took the rider's horse. I saw Gillacoemgain nod and wave the rider inside.

My husband stood then, alone on the frozen grass, reading the dispatch. When he finished reading, he looked into the sky overhead. I followed his gaze. Above, one of his falcons swirled in circles over Cawdor. It whistled to him.

Gillacoemgain crushed the paper in his hand then looked around the yard.

"Fergus!" he called, waving to the man.

At once, Fergus joined Gillacoemgain and they headed back into the castle.

As they passed under the window, a handful of words were caught in the wind and lifted to my window: *Malcolm. War. Macbeth.*

CHAPTER TWENTY

"*M*acbeth has escaped Malcolm's hold," Gillacoemgain was explaining when I entered his conference room later that day. So as not to interrupt the conversation, I settled into a seat along the wall in the back of the room. The clan leaders had already been assembled and riders had been departing Cawdor with messages since morning.

"How?" someone asked.

Gillacoemgain shook his head. "Malcolm is in England battling Cnut. I don't know how."

"Will he make for Inverness?" another of the lords asked.

"No. He is with Thorfinn of Orkney."

The room fell silent. The news was ominous. Thorfinn was Gillacoemgain's strongest opponent in the north. Gillacoemgain had barely subdued him these past months. If Macbeth was in league with Thorfinn, we would soon be at war.

"Let them come. Our men are ready," one of the clan leaders called.

"Have you heard from Mar?" another man asked.

"No," Gillacoemgain replied. "I'm waiting for word. Now we shall see who is loyal to Moray."

I listened as the men batted around names, who would remain loyal and who would turn. One thing was certain, Gillacoemgain did not know who his friends were. In that moment, I pitied him. All of Moray thought him a butcher. He had killed his brother, and many loathed him for it. If only they knew the reason why.

"What about Banquo of Lochaber?" someone asked, capturing my attention. "He's sworn his allegiance to you. He and Echmarcach of the isles will—"

"No," Gillacoemgain interrupted. "Lochaber's peace is false. He is allied with Thorfinn. They've been waiting for Macbeth's return."

My heart thundered in my chest. Gillacoemgain already knew. A million 'what ifs' rolled around in my mind. I shook my head. If they all only knew why Gilla-coemgain had killed Findelach, things would be different. But Gillacoemgain would never tell, would never disparage his sister's memory with such filth.

"Will Malcolm send reinforcements?" someone asked.

"He is at war in England. If he can, he will," Gillacoemgain answered, which was near the truth. If he wanted to, he would. But if Malcolm needed men in England, Moray was on her own.

I cast my gaze around the room. When I did so, however, my head felt dizzy. The air around me seemed to buzz, and I thought I heard Andraste whisper. *Damned.*

All at once, the room seemed to erupt into flame. The walls flooded with fire. Black smoke filled the room, ash falling like snow from above. I heard men screaming and felt the hot licks of fire on my skin. In the middle of the inferno, I saw Gillacoemgain, his face full of anguish. He called my name. Then, the flames ravaged him. Before my eyes, he burned until he was nothing more than ash.

I screamed.

"My Lady," someone said, shaking my shoulder. "Lady Gruoch?"

"Move back," I heard Gillacoemgain call.

I squeezed my eyes shut. I didn't want to see the fire, the ash. The flames felt so real. I felt their heat on my skin. I smelled the smoke. Gasping for air, I felt the press of people around me step aside as Gillacoemgain drew close.

"Gruoch?" Gillacoemgain whispered, taking my hand.

I realized then I was lying on the floor.

Afraid that I would see a burned man, I didn't open my eyes. I shook my head.

"Corbie? What happened? Are you all right?" Gilla-coemgain asked.

"She must have heard the conversation, took a fright," Fergus said softly.

"No," Gillacoemgain answered. "Boite's daughter doesn't fear war. Corbie?"

Finally, I opened my eyes to find Gillacoemgain looking down at me. His forehead was wrinkled with worry.

I exhaled deeply. The vision had passed. "I'm okay," I replied, offering my other hand so Gillacoemgain could help me up.

"Someone get her maid," Fergus called.

"What happened?" Gillacoemgain asked.

I shook my head. I didn't want to say.

"My Lady?" I heard Ute call. She arrived a moment later with Thora hot on her heels.

"Take Lady Gruoch to her chamber to rest," Gilla-coemgain told her then turned to me. "Should I come now? Do you need me?"

"No. It was nothing. Just...it was nothing. You have important work to do here."

Gillacoemgain nodded then saw me to the door.

"Come now, My Lady. Oh, my sister used to have fits something terrible when she was pregnant. All manner of things would set her off. Let's have a rest," Ute told me.

As we walked away, I heard Fergus' voice. He spoke

in a low tone to Gillacoemgain. "Like a banshee wail. You know what they used to say about her father. Ill-omened."

For a moment, Gillacoemgain did not reply. Then I heard him say, "It is for the gods to decide."

"Then let's hope they are on our side," Fergus said, closing the door behind them.

I hoped Fergus was right, because when I looked down at my clothes, I realized they were covered in ash.

For the next few weeks, messengers rode in and out of Cawdor. The Lord of Moray had his supporters, but it wasn't clear if he had enough. With Thorfinn backing Macbeth, and the west of Scotland with divided loyalties, it was unclear if Gillacoemgain had the men he needed. Much depended on Malcolm. And I knew, better than many, that Malcolm could not be trusted.

"I need to get you out of Cawdor," Gillacoemgain told me one night as he settled into bed beside me. "Spies are reporting that Thorfinn is amassing his naval army. I want you far away from any place near the water. We are too close to the Moray Firth here. You're in too fragile of a state. If Cawdor is overrun and you are taken by force, neither you nor the babes may survive. No matter what happens, I must see you and my children safe. Malcolm has sent word that he is preparing forces to head north to support me. He's inquired on your welfare. He told me to send you to Aberdeen."

"Aberdeen? It's right on the coast."

"That's right," Gillacoemgain said, a knowing look in his eyes.

My heart started beating hard. Malcolm wanted me somewhere easy to retrieve. If Gillacoemgain fell, Malcolm wanted to pluck me out of the middle of the fray and put me where he wanted me next. From Aberdeen, I could easily be bundled up and sent south… to Duncan? Was that Malcolm's plan for me if Gillacoemgain failed?

"No," I said. "Send me to my aunt. I'll go back amongst my women where I will be hidden and can safely deliver the babies."

"Malcolm…"

"Malcolm be damned. We both know his motives."

Gillacoemgain nodded. "We'll send word to Madelaine in secret. I'll tell Malcolm you will be sent to Aberdeen. You must ride south. War is coming, just as our little ones are ready to join this world. I must get you somewhere safe," he said, setting his hands on my stomach. "Gruoch," he said, looking carefully at me. "That day in the meeting room…what did you see? What vision?"

I shook my head. I didn't want to tell him. "It was nothing."

He touched my chin. "I know what you are. I've known it all along. Highland blood. The old blood thunders in your veins. Tell me. What did you see?"

"Fire."

"Pray to the Goddess. Pray to her. She will listen to you," he said then pulled me against him. "I love you, little raven."

"I love you too," I replied, swallowing the anguished moan that wanted to escape my lips.

CHAPTER TWENTY-ONE

*T*wo nights later, I found myself wide awake as the moon rose high in the sky. Macbeth. Who was this man to come and rip my world apart? Sighing, I looked back at Gillacoemgain who was sleeping soundly. The little chamber was warm, soft orange light pouring like liquid amber across the room, shining down on my husband.

Wrapping a shawl around me, I rose and stood over him. How handsome he looked in the firelight. I closed my eyes and imagined how he'd looked that summer day in the field with the falcons, smiling as the sun shone in golden hues on his hair.

Gillacoemgain grimaced in his sleep, then turned and rolled over.

I sighed then set my hands on my stomach. We expected word from Madelaine to come at any time.

Soon, I would ride south. This late in my pregnancy, it would be a difficult journey, but one I had to make. Malcolm wanted me within his reach. This time, I had more futures than my own to think of. Growing within me were the heirs of Moray, little ones who would, through me, have a claim to the throne of Scotland. I had to keep them safe.

Frowning, I went back to the fireplace. I lifted another log to drop on the flames but jumped when I saw an image dance across the surface of the water in the cauldron hanging there. I looked inside. The room around me suddenly grew distant, and I found myself standing along the shore. Moonlight glimmered on the waves. I wasn't sure where I was, but the smallest flakes of snow swirled in the air around me. Overhead, I looked to see the sky was alive with color. Streaks of purple, indigo, and golden light rolled across the starry canvas.

Startling me, I heard someone speak. I turned to find a man kneeling on the ground, his sword before him, hilt end up. His words were soft.

"May all that is to be come to pass through you. Amen," he whispered then rose.

When he did, I found myself standing face to face with my raven-haired man.

"You," he whispered.

How long had it been since I'd seen him? He looked older, but still as handsome as ever. The aurora of light overhead shimmered on his armor, casting incandescent hues on his pale face.

I reached out, wondering if I could touch him, but realized then I was little more than spirit. Quite by accident, I walked between the worlds. When I sought to speak, I heard only the raven's cry.

He gasped and backed away, a startled expression on his face.

His reaction caught me off guard, and I was flung back into myself. Once more I was in my chamber with Gillacoemgain. Sharp pains struck my temples. I sat, holding my head, hoping to ward off the terrible pain and tremor that sometimes followed. Not now. Not while I was so heavy with child.

I inhaled and exhaled deeply, blowing the pain away. My raven-haired man. It had been so long since I'd seen him last. My king, Andraste had once called him. Perhaps he was, but not in this lifetime. Perhaps he, like Banquo, belonged to a life lived long ago. Was he anything more than a buried memory come to life again? Did I walk the edges of time to join him? I didn't know.

I looked down at my hands, studying the lines thereon. Gruoch, Lady of Moray, daughter of Boite and Emer. Boudicca reborn. Who was I really? I stared into the flames. If the otherworld had never touched me, if I'd never gone to the coven, or to Ynes Verleath, what kind of woman would I have been? I glanced back at Gillacoemgain. I would be his wife, undistracted by visions of the otherworld. But when I looked back at my hands once more, I saw the now-faded scar on my palm, evidence that my soul knew and loved another before Gillacoemgain. And along with that scar, I saw the cut I'd made with my own knife, slicing my bind in half. Banquo was gone. My raven-haired man was some spirit who lived in a different world, a different time.

I closed my eyes and tried not to think about what would come next. I tried to think only of Gillacoemgain and the little ones growing inside me. Soon. They would be here soon. And so would Thorfinn and Macbeth. I could only pray that I had enough strength to endure them all.

❧

Forces amassed all around Cawdor as Gillacoemgain's army prepared to ride north into Orkney and Caithness. Tents popped up in the fields all around the castle as the first snow began to fall. It was a bitter cold morning when a familiar shape rode through the castle gates.

Gillacoemgain and I had been passing through the yard when Tavis arrived.

"Gruoch," he called, dismounting.

He was road-weary, but a look of relief flashed across his face as soon as he spotted me. My heart felt happy to see him. In truth, Tavis had been in my life for as long as

I could remember. He might have been Madelaine's champion, but he'd always watched over me like a father. In that, he was dear to me.

"Tavis," I called in reply and we turned to meet him.

He dismounted then kissed me on my cheek in greeting. "Well met. I come with Madelaine's apologies for the delay. The path is clear. We can ride whenever you're ready," he said but then looked at my stomach. "Gruoch…such a trip may be very dangerous," he said then looked at Gillacoemgain.

The expression on Gillacoemgain's face startled me. I could read very plainly then that he, too, was worried. If he left me at Cawdor I was not safe. If he sent me to Aberdeen I was not safe. If I rode south I was not safe.

"I'll be all right," I told them both. "Kelpie is a sturdy horse. He never shies at anything. I can make the trip."

"A wagon, maybe?" Tavis asked Gillacoemgain.

I shook my head. "It will attract too much attention."

Gillacoemgain frowned. "I'll send Standish and two other of my best men with you."

"But you need them here."

"No," Gillacoemgain said, "I *need* you safe. There is time."

I sighed then turned to Tavis. "Please take your rest. Eat, drink, and sleep if you can. I'll need to get ready," I told him then waved to one of the lads crossing the square. "Will you escort my guest to the main hall?"

"Yes, My Lady," the boy said.

I took the reins of Tavis' horse. "I'll have him fed."

Tavis nodded. "Just let me know when you're ready," he said then followed the boy inside.

Gillacoemgain patted Tavis' horse on the neck. "It will be a difficult trip," he told me then. "I...I don't know."

I looped my arm in his, and together, we led Tavis' horse to the stables. I passed the steed off to the master of horse then wordlessly led Gillacoemgain back to the mews where his falcons waited.

Almost instantly, he smiled then whistled playfully at the birds. They responded by turning an eye toward him, hopping across the mew to get close to him. They were keen to fly, and happy, or so it seemed, to see him.

"You'll have to teach our sons how to hunt with them, when they're old enough," I told him. I wanted Gillacoemgain to have faith in the future. I needed the reassurance as well.

Gillacoemgain smiled at me. "Sons now, is it?" He set his hand on my stomach.

"We'll soon see."

Gillacoemgain reached for me, taking my face into his hands. He pulled me into a deep kiss and after, set his forehead against mine.

"Think of the summer. Think of the sunshine. We'll all be together. All four of us...and your birds and Thora too. We will roam the hills together. Think of your sons' laughter. Make the dream real, then lock it in your heart.

If darkness comes, close your eyes and remember the dream," I whispered.

"Corbie," he whispered, setting the lightest kiss on my forehead.

"Gillacoemgain?" a voice called. We turned to see Fergus. He was holding a scroll. "Sorry, My Lord, My Lady. News from King Malcolm."

Gillacoemgain smiled at me then touched my chin.

"Go ahead," I told him. "I'll come in a moment."

He nodded then turned and joined Fergus.

I waited a few more moments, gazing out at the tents covering the field. I was not surprised when Eochaid arrived. In truth, I'd been waiting for him.

"Lady Gruoch," he said with a smile. "You'll be traveling south then?" he asked.

"Yes," I replied. "And you, you are not planning on marching with the men, are you?"

"No, M'Lady, I'll stay here and keep watch on M'Lord's falcons."

"Good. Eochaid...I don't know what will happen. If Cawdor gets overrun...make sure you stay safe, stay away. But please know, wherever I am, you are welcomed to join me. You can ride south with me, if you'd like."

Eochaid cocked his head, and I knew he was listening to the invisible fairy man, but he simply said, "No, M'Lady. But thank you."

"May the fair ones watch over you," I said, gently squeezing his shoulder.

"And over you too," he said, but then he had a confused expression on his face. "I don't understand, but he, Eitri," he said, motioning to his shoulder, "told me to tell you to lock the dream in your heart as well. Does that make sense to you?"

"Yes," I said, trying to hold back the tears that threatened. Gently, I hugged the boy then turned and left, a heavy feeling of dread sweeping over my heart.

CHAPTER TWENTY-TWO

I headed back to my chamber where I found Ute pacing pensively.

"My Lady? Lord Gillacoemgain told me to prepare your things. We're riding for Aberdeen?"

"Yes," I lied, "as King Malcolm commands."

She nodded. "I've packed warm clothes for us and the little ones," she said. Her voice sounded assured, but she had gone completely pale.

"Very well. Head to the kitchens and ensure we have enough food for us and four men for the journey."

"Yes, My Lady," she said then headed out of the chamber.

I opened my trunk and pulled out what few belongings I could not bear the thought of parting with. I set Uald's gift on the bed, as well as the torcs and amulet I'd brought with me from Ynes Verleath. I gazed down at the violet-colored wedding gown lying in the bottom on the trunk. It would have to stay behind. Sighing, I closed the trunk then dug into my medicines, pulling out anything that might help me in case anything went wrong during the journey. I placed everything into my bag then sat down on the bed. The little ones turned excitedly. How was I ever going to manage the trip?

The door opened behind me. Gillacoemgain entered.

"I spoke to Tavis. I want you on your way today. The men are getting ready. They will be ready when you are."

I nodded, rose, then pulled some warm clothes from my wardrobe. Slowly, I began getting dressed, Gillacoemgain helping me slide into a woolen tunic. Wordlessly, he bent and helped me lace up my riding boots.

I lifted Uald's gift, but the belt wouldn't fit around my waist. The tension was so high, the air so thick and sad between us, that we were startled when we both laughed.

"Here," Gillacoemgain said, helping me strap the sword around my chest. "It's harder to pull the blade when it's on your back but is still at hand if needed. And take this as well," he said, unbelting the dagger he always wore. I recognized it by the gold pommel decorated with a Pictish flower.

I shook my head. "Oh no. It's such a precious blade. You should carry it."

Gillacoemgain took my hand and placed the dagger in my palm. "It bears the symbol of my mother's line which, much like your own, springs from the royal blood of this land. It was given to my sister by my mother, and before her, by her mother, all the way back to our ancestors from the isle of Scáthach where the women in my family once learned the ancient arts."

I stared at Gillacoemgain. "Then you do know," I whispered.

"From the moment I laid eyes on you, walking into Madelaine's hall like an ancient queen. And I know, no matter what happens to me, you will survive. And you will care for our children."

I closed my eyes, wishing for the millionth time that the babes I carried were, in fact, his. Tears streamed down my cheeks.

Gillacoemgain wiped my tears. "None of that, little Corbie," he whispered. Taking the dagger, he slid it into its scabbard then slipped it into the top of my boot, lacing it inside.

Without another word, we headed downstairs where Ute, Tavis, Standish, and two soldiers waited.

Gillacoemgain nodded to Tavis, and we all headed outside where Kelpie waited, already saddled.

With Tavis' and Gillacoemgain's help, I mounted my beloved animal while Thora wove between the horses, excited to go on a new adventure. I hated how useless I felt. My sole concern had to be for my children, but in days past I could fight just as well as any man. I had my own sword, and I knew how to use it. Rather than running, I should have been at Gillacoemgain's side. Instead of fighting, I was leaving my husband to...I didn't want to think of what. The vision I'd seen wanted to impose itself on me. I closed the door to it, not wanting to remember.

I pulled the heavy cloak I wore around me tightly as I settled onto Kelpie. It was going to be a long, uncomfortable ride. As long as Kelpie stayed sure-footed and we avoided trouble, everything would be fine.

Gillacoemgain helped Ute onto her horse, settling her in, then spoke in low tones with Standish. After, he returned to me.

"Gillacoe—" I began, reaching out to touch his face.

"No goodbyes," he said, taking my hand, kissing my fingers. "Ride safe, and I'll join you and my little ones very soon." But even as he said it, I knew we both felt the dark shadow that hung over us.

I closed my eyes. I wanted to be with him in that moment, but the raven showed me pictures. I saw Gillacoemgain in the middle of a roundhouse. Once more, I felt the heat from flames licking the walls and saw fire and ash breaking through the ceiling.

I gasped.

"Corbie?" *All will burn. Make your heart ready, Cerridwen.*

Shaking, I opened my eyes and looked at him. "Beware...beware the flames...beware of roundhouses."

"Roundhouses?"

"I saw...flames. A meeting place...there was fire all around you."

Gillacoemgain studied me closely, his forehead furrowing. "Don't think of it. Try to think of a name for our little ones."

I smiled weakly. "You'll let me choose?" I asked as cheerfully as I could, still frozen by the image of fire that had danced across my mind.

"If we have a daughter, name her Crearwy, for my sister?"

Tears threatened. I swallowed hard. "Of course."

He reached out to stroke my cheek one last time then let me go. "I love you, Corbie," he told me in a low voice so the others could not hear.

"I love you too," I whispered. "May the Morrigu ride at your side."

"And at yours," he said then stepped back, motioning to Standish that we were ready.

Taking the reins, I turned Kelpie and followed the other riders across the ward to the gate. I looked back just once more.

Gillacoemgain raised his hand in farewell.

I gazed at him long and hard, trying to engrain his image into my mind, hoping it was not true, but still knowing I would never see Gillacoemgain of Moray again.

CHAPTER TWENTY-THREE

*W*e started our slow trek south. Kelpie seemed to know he had an important task and rode as gently as if he were a lady's palfrey, not the charger Boite had bought as a gift for his daughter. We rode late into the night, stopping in a thick glen. The canopy of trees overhead kept out the light snow that fell.

"How are you, Lady?" Standish asked me as he helped me dismount.

My heart had been struck numb the moment I rode from Cawdor. I felt like everything inside me was frozen. I felt nothing. My body, however, told a different tale. I was exhausted. When I slid off Kelpie, all I wanted was to close my eyes and rest. "Just a bit tired," I said.

Tavis had already gotten to work laying a bear skin on the ground at the base of a wide old oak tree.

"Will you rest?" he asked.

I stretched my back. It ached terribly. I nodded.

"Here, My Lady," Ute said as she and Tavis gently lowered me to the ground.

Tavis set about lighting a fire while Ute dug through her things and handed me a sweet cake.

"Will you eat, My Lady?"

I shook my head. "I'll sleep a bit," I told her, then tried to settle in. Soon, the fire was crackling. Thora came and lay down beside me, setting her head on my leg.

Tavis sat beside me as Gillacoemgain's men rested. "How many nights I camped by that stream, waiting for Madelaine to return. That old bear kept me warm more times than I can count," he said as he warmed his hands by the fire.

"You've always been so good to us," I whispered, feeling my eyes drift closed.

"She is the love of my life," he told me. "I would do anything for her…or those she loves."

I reached out and patted Tavis on the arm. I didn't want to hear more. His words made the ice around my heart crack. I didn't want to feel.

My eyes closed, and I slept.

That night, I dreamed of Gillacoemgain. We were standing in the sunny field, his falcons flying overhead. He was laughing as he carried a dark-haired girl on his shoulders. I looked down to see the same child I'd had a vision of once before was holding my hand.

I smiled at him, leaning down to kiss him on his brow.

"What is it, Mother?" he asked.

I shook my head. "Nothing."

"What's that?" the little girl called.

I turned to look at a strange orange light rolling across the horizon. Slowly, Gillacoemgain lowered the girl off his shoulders and handed her to me. He pulled his sword and stepped in front of us just as a wave of fire crashed across the field, burning everything in its path.

"Get back," he told me.

I took the little ones then turned and ran from the flames. I stopped just a moment to look back, long enough to see my husband stand before the fire, sword drawn. And like a wave, the flames washed over him.

Gasping, I woke with a start.

Ute and Thora both slept soundly beside me.

"Are you all right, My Lady?" one of the soldiers asked. I realized he'd been standing guard.

"Just a dream," I said, trying to shake the horrible image.

He nodded. "Almost morning. Time to get going anyway."

He roused the others. In near silence, we ate a meager breakfast then departed once more. Kelpie carried me safely through the forest and across the fields, and at the end of the second day, we rode into the familiar valley of Madelaine's keep.

"Welcome home," Tavis told me.

My back ached. Cold and hungry as I was, never had such a hated place been a more welcomed sight.

We rode into the yard and there we dismounted. At once, Thora disappeared into the main hall. There was a flurry of excitement as servants rushed to meet us. Tavis instructed them to provision the Moray men for the return home.

"Thank the Mother Goddess you've arrived," Madeline said, rushing across the yard to greet us as she pulled a cloth around her. As soon as she caught sight of Tavis, Madelaine sighed in relief. She pulled me into the embrace. "Oh, my dear sweet thing, how are you?"

"As well as can be expected."

"Come," Madelaine said, interrupting my thoughts. "You must be weary. Corbie…you're huge!"

"Twins," I whispered to her under my breath.

"These are dangerous hours," she said, a worried expression crossing her pretty features. "We need to get you to Epona. Fife left for Edinburgh yesterday. He didn't want to be here when you arrived. The more he didn't know, the better. We can leave for the coven first thing in the morning."

I nodded, and we all headed into the great hall. The servants moved about busily gathering supplies and no sooner had we arrived than Standish came to take my leave.

"Won't you stay the night?" I asked. "It's bitter cold."

"No, My Lady. We need to get back to his lordship."

I nodded. The desperation of the situation was painfully apparent. Moray would be won or lost in this battle. Gillacoemgain needed every man he had. And even that would not be enough. I had to try to do something. After all, if he died…no, I would not think of it.

"May the Great Mother see you safely returned," I told him.

"And you safely delivered," he replied with a smile. "Be safe, Lady Gruoch," he said, a serious expression on his face.

"Thank you. And you."

He nodded.

With that, the Moray men headed out of the castle and back to Gillacoemgain.

"What can I get for you?" Madelaine asked me as she rubbed my back and shoulders. "Do you want a bath? Something to eat?"

"All I want is sleep."

"I have a room prepared for you," she replied, motioning to a serving girl.

"You'll see to Ute and Thora?"

Madelaine nodded, lent me her arm, then we headed upstairs. I exhaled deeply. It felt good to be back in Madelaine's care.

Upstairs, I entered a chamber already warmed by a cheery fire. Madelaine helped me re-dress then lowered me into bed, covering me.

"No fever," she said, checking my forehead.

"No, I'm only tired."

"Sleep, little raven," she whispered, gently kissing my forehead. A moment later, I heard the chamber door close behind her.

I closed my eyes. My thoughts sprang at once to Gillacoemgain.

"Dark lady, protect him," I whispered as I fell asleep.

Just as I drifted off, I heard a reply come in a whisper. *No.*

CHAPTER TWENTY-FOUR

We rose early the following morning and headed out. The sun had barely risen over the horizon. Fat snowflakes fell. The ruby red of the sun cast a rosy blush on the snow. Kelpie's deep breaths cast clouds of fog as we headed into the woods. We rode slowly. My body was already sore from the long ride, and I felt a terrible strain in my groin. I rode wincing at every bump. If I had waited in Moray even another day, I would not have made it on time.

As was our habit, we stopped at the stream to bid Tavis farewell.

"My thoughts will be with you," Tavis told me.

"Thank you. Please, stay warm. You'll send Uald to check on him?" I asked Madelaine who nodded.

"I have my bear fur," he told me.

I nodded, but as I looked closely at Tavis, I recognized that he wasn't the young man he once was. His days of sleeping on the cold ground should come to a close.

Madelaine and Tavis embraced, kissing goodbye, then my aunt and I headed deep into the forest.

Our slow pace made the ride cumbersome. Finally giving up, I asked Madelaine to help me dismount. Thora, too excited to wait, ran ahead.

"It hurts," I told her, wincing as a terrible ache gripped me.

"Too much riding. It wasn't safe," Madelaine said, the look of frustration on her face evident as she helped me slowly slide off.

"It could not be helped. I wasn't safe in Cawdor."

"But Gillacoemgain's forces are riding north."

"And Macbeth's and Thorfinn's are riding south."

Madelaine frowned, worry marring her features. "Was Moray...doesn't Gillacoemgain have the support he needs? Isn't Malcolm sending reinforcements?"

I stopped to catch my breath, wincing as I pressed my fists into my lower back. I gazed at the snow-covered limbs hanging over me. The forest really did look beautiful. The morning light had given way to soft slants of light. I closed my eyes and took a deep breath, inhaling the scents of pine and snow.

"Did you ever stop to wonder how Macbeth escaped?" I asked Madelaine.

"Macbeth?"

"How could Malcolm's ward slip away so easily? How is it that Macbeth was able to find his way home and rally those opposed to Gillacoemgain? When my husband sought his allies, he found many were already arming to cut him down. How could that have happened? How could a single man, without a father, an army, or an estate—save that ruled by Gillacoemgain —manage it?"

"Do you think Malcolm...that Malcolm sent Macbeth north? Against Gillacoemgain?"

"I think that Malcolm wants what he wants, when he wants it, and he is apt to change his mind. Malcolm told Gillacoemgain to send me to Aberdeen."

"But that would put you on the coast."

"Easy pickings...for Duncan."

Madelaine shook her head. "My half-brother...he is nothing like Boite and me. We will pray to the Goddess that Gillacoemgain survives. I see in your eyes that you've come to love him. For your sake, for your children's, and for Scotland, we'll pray for his victory."

I reached out and squeezed Madelaine's hand. Snowflakes fell on her red hair. How like a fey thing she looked in the winter woods. "Where do you get that red hair?" I asked my aunt, dusting the snowflakes away.

"My father," she said. While Madelaine, Boite, and Malcolm had all shared a mother, Aelfgifu, Madelaine's father had died young, freeing up her mother to marry Kenneth II. "I remember him just a little. I was very

young when he died. But I remember his big red beard."
She smiled wistfully, lost in her thoughts.

"What was your mother like?" I asked her as we
moved forward once more through the snow.

Madelaine smiled. "When she was young, she was
full of laughter. From what I remember, she was very
happy married to my father. But Malcolm's and Boite's
father, Kenneth, was not an easy man. I think some of the
light went out inside her when she married him."

"As it does for many women," I said.

"Yes," Madelaine said absently. "But not with you,
my little raven. It seems, despite your apprehension,
Gillacoemgain and you found your way."

"He was not the man many thought he was."

"Then we shall pray all the more for him. Come," she
said, taking my arm. "Let's get you settled before you
birth your little ones in the snow.

It was not long after that I saw Thora darting through
the woods, Uald following behind her.

"When I saw Thora, I thought I'd better check on
you," she told us. "Corbie, are you carrying a litter?" she
asked with a laugh.

"Perhaps I carry a babe of the high hills. Such great
men have not been seen in a thousand years. I thought it
was time to rekindle their blood."

Uald chuckled then took Kelpie's reins. Working
slowly, we finally made it to the coven by midday.

The little space was covered in a blanket of snow.

Smoke puffed out of the small chimneys—including Sid's. I was happy and relieved to learn she was there.

The sound of the horses and Thora's happy barks caught everyone's attention. No sooner had we arrived than Epona and Sid emerged from Epona's house.

Sid smiled at me, shaking her head. "Looks like my bed is the only one that will fit her. Might as well put her stuff in there," she told Uald.

"Oh Cerridwen," Epona said, looking worried. "How are you?"

"Tired and achy."

"The ride from Moray?"

"Kelpie did his best. It was a long ride, but we made it."

"Once Uald gets your things settled, I'd like to examine you."

I nodded wearily.

"Sweet friend," Sid said, setting her hand on my stomach. "Come," she said, leading me to her little cabin. Madelaine followed behind us. The moment I stepped into the little cabin, it was like I'd stepped into liquid heat. The room was bathed in the cheery orange glow of the firelight. The logs on the fire popped and crackled. I was relieved to be out of the cold. Once inside, I could also see that her cabin was already ready. She had a cot made up for herself, and the bed ready for me. She'd been expecting me all along. With a heavy sigh, I sat down on the bed and started peeling off my heavy riding clothes. My body hurt. The little ones were pressing down so hard I felt like they were going to come out at any moment. At the same time, I could barely breathe.

"Rest," Sid told me then turned to Madelaine. "I'll stay with her if you want to get settled in."

Madelaine nodded. "Be back soon," she said then headed out.

"Off to Uald," Sid said, watching her out the window. "And you are here with me once more."

"I'm half here," I replied, my eyes closing.

"That's the way of it. The days close to the end are the hardest. And with two, you must ache miserably."

For more than she knew. *Gillacoemgain.* I lay down, forcing the thoughts away. I must have fallen asleep, because I woke sometime after dark to the sound of Epona's voice.

"Cerridwen?" she said gently, shaking my shoulder.

"Epona?"

"You've been sleeping. May I examine you?" she asked.

Disoriented, I looked around. Sid was sitting on the bed beside me.

"Yes," I said groggily. Sid sat holding my hand while Epona cared for me.

"Within the week for certain, but more likely it will be only a matter of days," she pronounced after a bit. "There is no sign of injury from the ride. We are lucky."

I sighed and closed my eyes. All I wanted was sleep.

And more than that, I wanted my husband. Where was Gillacoemgain that night? Was he already marching north to, all signs seemed to suggest, his certain doom? A tear slid down my cheek.

"Let me know if she needs anything," Epona said to Sid.

"Of course," Sid said softly as she laid another blanket over me.

I heard the door open and close as Epona left. Once more, Sid sat down beside me and took my hand. She bent and set a soft kiss on my forehead. "You're safe here. Let go," she whispered.

I feel asleep a moment later.

❧

J woke to thin rays of morning sunlight slanting through the window shutters, illuminating the motes that floated in the air. Sleepily, I raised my hand and chased them through the space.

"Are you saying my house is dusty?" Sid asked.

"Glimmering," I replied. "Speaking of, where is Nadia?"

"Banished. The good neighbors don't do well with human childbirth. Have you thought of names for your little ones?" Sid asked.

"Crearwy, for a girl, after Gillacoemgain's sister."

"He has a sister?"

"She died," I replied, the image of Gillacoemgain with orange-colored blood stains on his hands fleeting through my mind.

Sid nodded thoughtfully. "And if they are boys?"

"I'm at a loss."

Sid laughed. "Boy's names are always difficult. I struggled for a name for my son as well. His father chose his name."

"What is it?"

"Eochaid."

I sat up and looked at Sid. "Eochaid?"

She smiled. "He's a sweet little thing with a mop of brown curls. His eyes are much like mine. He's happy in the otherworld with his father, but I miss him terribly."

She didn't know. Her son had been with me all this time. Why? Had the fey sent the boy to keep watch over me? My heart twisted. Should I tell her? I wasn't sure.

"It's a lovely name," I said, deciding it was best not to interfere with the business of the good neighbors. I was sorry then, however, that I hadn't done more for the boy. I would see to him the moment I returned to Moray.

"We'll think of something for your little ones. Maybe there will be two girls," Sid replied.

I smiled, thinking how cute two little lasses would be. But it struck me that it would be Malcolm—or worse— Duncan, who ruled the course of their lives. The idea of it filled me with rage.

There was a knock on the door. Epona stuck her head inside. "Ah, awake? Want to walk around a bit?"

It was the last thing I wanted to do, but I knew well enough that if I wanted the babes to come, it would help.

I nodded. "Coming," I told her. With Sid's help, I rose to get dressed.

Despite the fact that I felt like my children might come any moment, they did not arrive that day or the next. Ankles swelled to the size of tree trunks, feeling like I could barely breathe, and my emotions beginning to overflow, the hours before the little ones arrived were harrowing. I sat awake early one morning staring at the flames in Sid's fireplace.

I was about to give birth to Duncan's children.

It was the truth.

It was a pain I had buried.

Returning once more to the coven, to the sights and smells of a place I loved so well, so far removed from the comfort of Moray, and so close to the very forest where I'd been a victim to my cousin's lust, the lies I'd told myself wore thin. If I had not met Duncan in the woods, I would be pregnant with Gillacoemgain's children. The babes I carried would have been born of two loving parents. Duncan had robbed me of much that day. He'd taken my body, my dignity, and stolen my womb for his own use. It was not the fault of the little ones within me. They were innocent. But Duncan, the man who had helped himself to whatever he pleased, was destined to one day be King of Scotland. My cousin. My kin. Why had Malcolm asked for me to be sent to Aberdeen? Did my uncle wish me to be the next Queen of Scots? I shuddered at the thought. Would Malcolm really try to marry me to Duncan if Gillacoemgain fell? Andraste and Aridmis had both prophesied I would be Queen. Was that how? Would the babes in my womb help to seal Duncan's power over Moray? It was a smart and disgusting move. Believing I carried Moray's heirs, would Malcolm kill Gillacoemgain, then Macbeth, leaving Duncan to stand alone at the top of the heap? With the Lady of Moray and Moray's heirs at his side, Duncan would win it all. The move was grotesque and exactly the kind of thing Malcolm was capable of orchestrating.

As I stared into the flames, tears rolled down my cheeks. I chided myself for my sadness. It was not sorrow I needed. It was anger. Revenge. The raven within me shrieked for vengeance. But I had to wait. The time wasn't right. I could feel it in my bones. One day, I would take my revenge on Duncan. But not here. And not now. But when?

Frustrated with myself, I left Sid sleeping and pulled on my heavy robe. Walking carefully on the slick snow, I went to the little cabin Aridmis and Druanne shared and knocked on the door.

Aridmis smiled at me when she answered. "I was

expecting you," she said. "Druanne is off distilling herbs. Come in."

"You were expecting me?" I asked.

She nodded. "Of course. Your little ones. I'm sure you are curious to know their fates."

I looked at my old friend. Her curly golden hair looked the same, but there were lines around her eyes and mouth that were not there before. The years were working on her as they were on me. "No," I said. "I...I want to know what is to come. My children will be safe with me."

"Will they?" Aridmis asked absently as she shifted some papers on her table. She smiled softly at me. "There is much on your horizon."

"Yes. Please tell me, will Gillacoemgain live? Will Macbeth win the north from him? What of Duncan?"

Aridmis frowned then said, "Some believe our fate is in our stars, but many times our faults are not in our stars but in ourselves. Soon, you will have to make choices that will wound you. Choose wisely. Choose what feels right in your heart. If you do that, good things shall come to pass."

"And if I make the wrong choice?"

"What is the wrong choice? How will you ever know?"

"You riddle like someone else I know."

"You speak of the Wyrds."

"Yes."

"And what do they say on the matter?"

Hover through the fog, the snow, the filthy air. There to meet with Macbeth. "Little I can understand."

Aridmis smiled. "I've met your sisters a few times. They have their own ways. In the end, your choices are your own to make. Choose wisely."

I nodded. The first rays of morning sunlight shimmered into the room. "Breakfast?" I asked her.

She shook her head. "Fasting."

"Thank you, Aridmis."

"For riddles?" she asked with a smile.

"For...for reminding me that I can choose."

She nodded and opened up the door once more.

"I can tell you one thing you will like to hear," she said as I stepped out into the snowy square.

I raised an eyebrow at her.

She set her hand on my stomach. "A boy and a girl. Both healthy."

I set my hand on hers. "Thank you."

She let me go, nodded, and then went back inside.

I looked up at the sky. A hawk called as it flew over the coven then off into the forest.

"Gillacoemgain," I whispered. "May my love fly to you," I said then closed my eyes, trying to feel the thin space between the worlds, the space between him and me, wanting him to feel me. I dare not cast to him, but I wanted him to know how much I loved him. In that small moment, I sensed my husband. I surrounded him with my love, then felt it reflect back to me. But in that strange empty space to which I'd opened myself, I felt more love than just Gillacoemgain's. There was another voice in the ether, another spirit that sought me, and I knew his nature like I knew myself. Banquo.

Cerridwen?

I pulled back, forcing myself away from him. I opened my eyes, planting myself in the real world once more. The wound on my heart strained. I would not think of Banquo. Not then. Not now. Never again.

"Cerridwen," Bride called as she stepped out of her house. "I've got a taste for elderberries this morning. Come, let's see what Epona has in storage."

Moving slowly, I joined Bride, hooking my arm in hers. Together, we shuffled through the snow toward Epona's house.

Bride laughed. "Like two turtles racing."

I chuckled and wrapped the world around me like a blanket, insulating myself from the feeling that wanted to break my heart. A familiar ache crept across my head, threatening to explode. I steeled myself to it. Instead, I listened to the call of birds in the forest and the sound of Kelpie nickering as Uald chatted to him. I would not let the sorrow drown me.

The day passed slowly. My body ached with contractions. I felt like someone was knifing me in the back. When I lay down that night, my groin felt heavy, so I was not surprised when I woke in the middle of the night with labor pains. It was beginning.

"Sid," I gasped, realizing that my water had broken. My clothing and the blankets were wet.

Sid woke groggily. "Ugh, you could have waited until morning, at least, Raven Beak," she said with a laugh. "Let me go get Epona."

The pain lasted for hours, coming in sharp, shooting batches, but I was able to manage. Night passed into morning, and the sun climbed higher into the sky as the birthing pains racked me. Epona and Sid stayed with me the entire time, Madelaine coming in and out to check on me. Seeing me in pain, so it turned out, was too much for her to bear. Bride brought everyone food and drink, eyeing me sympathetically.

By the lunch hour, it was time.

"Help her," Epona told Sid who sat on the bed behind me, supporting my body. "Now, Cerridwen, comes the hard work. Do as I say."

I nodded, tears streaming down my cheeks. The pain was unbearable.

Epona checked me once more then nodded. "Good girl. Now we push," she told me. "Push with all your might."

I pushed hard, feeling like my body was breaking. I screamed.

Outside, Thora howled. In the midst of all the pain and confusion, her distress worried me. When I heard her, I flung myself from my body. I stood in shadow form outside Sid's house. I bent to comfort my dog.

"It will be all right," I told her.

Thora quieted and wagged her tail.

I saw that Madelaine and Uald were also waiting outside. Madelaine wept as she heard me cry out.

"She'll be okay," Uald reassured her. "She's a fighter."

"It's too dangerous, carrying two."

Uald shook her head. "Nothing will stop your niece. Nothing would dare."

I smiled at Uald then turned to go back. Before I did so, however, I noticed a strange, blurry spot on the hillside. The moment I saw it, I traveled to and through it, arriving once more at the cauldron terrace in Ynes Verleath. Andraste and Nimue stood waiting.

"Andraste?" I whispered.

"The legend of Cerridwen tells that the Goddess bore a son who was Taliesin. Yet, as we all know, Taliesin was Goddess-loved, thus he had a secret name. Can you guess it, Cerridwen?"

I shook my head. My soul was tired. I had lost so much energy in the birthing process. I heard Sid whisper *"come back"* into my ear.

Andraste smiled at me. "The Goddess called him Lulach. Go, child. Your babies await."

I turned away from Ynes Verleath, my raven's eyes spying the coven below me, but in the darkness far away,

I saw fire. I smelled smoke and felt the flames. And I heard screaming.

"Gruoch!" Gillacoemgain called. "Gruoch!"

"Gillacoemgain," I whispered. I moved to go to him.

"No," Sid yelled, appearing in her spirit guise before me. "No!" She grabbed my arm and pulled me roughly back toward my body.

I heard myself suck in a deep breath.

"Back. She's back," Sid said, sounding relieved

"Thank the Mother," Epona said, her words drowned out by a squalling voice. "Your daughter," she said, setting a wailing bundle in my hands.

"Oh Crearwy," I whispered, pressing my cheek against her head. "Oh, my poor sweet baby, your father is dead."

The women in the room were struck silent.

Through my tear-clouded eyes, I looked at Sid who picked up another bundle and handed it to me. "Your son."

Madelaine entered a moment after, clasping her hands before her mouth as she looked at me.

"A boy and a girl," I told her.

Weeping, Madelaine leaned over me and the little ones, kissing all of us.

While Crearwy cried, my baby boy looked around with squinty little eyes. "Hello, Lulach," I said, kissing him on the forehead. My emotions poured out of me, and I wept bitterly. I knew that Gillacoemgain was dead.

And he had died thinking he was leaving me and his children behind. I didn't know what was going to come next, but more than anything else, I knew I had to protect our children.

"Feisty gal," Sid said at last, bending over to kiss Crearwy. "Maybe try nursing her?" she suggested, gently taking Lulach from me.

"Come now, little lass," I told her, setting her to my breast. Luckily, she latched easily.

It was then that I saw that something had caught Sid's attention. She was looking from Lulach to the incorporeal air, seemingly listening to someone. Nadia.

"Yes," she whispered then added, "go ahead."

I squinted my eyes to see the fairy woman but was too exhausted.

Sid smiled at me. "She kissed him, put a blessing on him. Look," she said, touching Lulach between eyebrows where he now had a small red dart on his skin.

I nodded then lay my head back. I felt hot tears stream down my cheeks. My whole world had shifted out from under me in a single moment. I looked from Lulach to Crearwy then closed my eyes.

"Farewell," I whispered, hoping that if Gillacoemgain's spirit lingered nearby, he would hear.

CHAPTER TWENTY-FIVE

$\mathcal{I}$ spent the next few days recovering, mindful that I needed to return as soon as possible. If my vision was true, I needed to be ready. I had not meant to, but I'd fallen in love with Gillacoemgain. The idea that he was gone broke my heart. As Gillacoemgain's wife, I was able to forget that Duncan was truly my children's father. I could pretend. It was easy to play the part. With Gillacoemgain, I was the Lady of Moray. I was not a priestess or Boudicca or one of the Wyrd Sisters. My druid husband had not abandoned me. I was a woman loved by a man. And I, in turn, had loved my husband. It was a dream I'd slowly grown attached to, and now, it seemed, that dream was gone. Tears slid slowly down my cheeks, and I mourned the man I believed to be dead, and with him, my future. Now, I would have to face the truth. I was responsible, once more, for my vengeance. I was alone. And now, I had two small children who would rely on me to protect them like only the raven could.

One morning, I woke to cries. Lulach slept soundly while Crearwy called. I lifted her and began to nurse her. How different they were. Lulach was a very peaceful child. Crearwy, on the other hand, seemed to fuss at everything. Once she was eating, however, she turned peaceful. How sweet she looked, her dark hair curling around her tiny ears. I gently stroked her head, my eyes drifting closed once more. I was awoken a moment later when Epona entered.

"Sorry to wake you," she whispered, sitting down at the edge of the bed. She gazed at Crearwy, took a deep breath, then said, "We must talk."

"Is something wrong?"

Epona frowned, a worried expression on her face. "I…I had Uald fetch a wet nurse."

"You've brought an outsider here?" I stared at her.

She nodded.

"But there is no need. I can handle both of the children. It is tiring, but I can do it. Once I return, I'll have my maid to help me."

Epona was silent for a long time.

"What is it?"

"The future of this coven is of great importance to me. The old ways are dying out. Each year fewer and fewer young girls learn the ancient arts. Something must be done. I must ensure our way of life continues. I...I was given a vision. My successor must be someone who has been raised here from birth, someone trained in the old ways from a young age. That is the only way. The Mother herself revealed this to me. Crearwy...Crearwy is meant to succeed me, to take my place as Lady here. I have seen the future. It is destined."

"Crearwy?" I looked down at the child.

Epona nodded. "The night you told me what happened, the night you conceived your little ones, I saw a vision of your daughter here with us."

"Then you have brought the nurse, not to help me, but so I can leave Crearwy here."

"Yes."

"What if I don't want to leave Crearwy here?"

Epona was silent.

"Epona!"

"Cerridwen, Crearwy must remain here. The highland blood in your veins is full of magic. We will need your—and Crearwy's—help in order for the religion to survive. I know what I say is true. If you doubt me, ask Andraste. She knows what will be."

"You want me to give up my daughter?" I whispered.

"No. I want you to leave her in my care. Leave her here and Uald, Sid, and all the others will be her mother. We will love her and raise her and train her to be the next leader of this coven. She will grow up away from court life."

"I...but Epona, she's my daughter."

"Yes. And you can choose to free her of the obligations that have chained you. You can leave her to a life in service of the divine."

I stared at Epona.

"I...I know what I ask of you seems impossible. Let me leave you to think on it."

Epona rose and left me to my thoughts.

I looked down at Crearwy. The tiny baby cooed as she ate. She was pretty, pretty as any baby could be. As she ate, she opened and closed her tiny hands. I loved her with my whole heart. I loved her and Lulach more than I had ever loved anyone or anything.

Epona was asking for something I could not give. I could not give my daughter up to be raised by another, could I? But could I give her up to get her away from the intrigues of court? When Malcolm died, Duncan would rule over her fate. I couldn't stand the thought. I could offer her a better life than the one I'd been given. What was I to do? I could ask Andraste. If anyone knew what was destined, it was her. The Wyrds. It was Andraste's job to know. But she riddled. No, I would not ask Andraste. I would wait and go to the source.

*T*hat night, as the children slept under Sid's watchful care, I went outside. The winter wind whipped coldly. I went to the well and rested my head on the cold stones. I had planned to do a casting, to call the raven and seek the answers from the dark goddesses, but I was too tired. It would have to wait. I rose to go back inside but found Bride coming toward me.

"What do you need? I can fetch it for you," I called, concerned to find her in the chilly night air.

The wind blew her hood back and revealed a face that did not belong to Bride. The Crone. "Such a kind heart," she said.

I bowed my head. "Lady."

"You are right that Andraste riddles, and too much depends on the truth. Leave Crearwy with Epona. She is right. Crearwy is her successor. The women of your line belong to the Goddess. The men belong to the world," the Crone said then turned to leave.

"What else doesn't Andraste tell me?" I called against the wind.

"A woman who calls back the Goddess of Death," the Crone said with a laugh. "For your courage, I will answer you. While Epona has waited for Crearwy, Andraste has waited for you."

"For me?"

"As her successor."

"But how?"

The sound of a door swinging open caught both my and the Goddess' attention. Bride. Clutching her wrap, Bride stepped outside.

"Heard my voice, did you? Not yet," the Crone told Bride and then walked into the darkness where she disappeared.

Bride and I exchanged glances. Bride shook her head then went back inside. I headed back into Sid's house. Sid was dozing peacefully in a chair by the fire.

I sat down on the side of the bed and stared at my children. I was the one Andraste waited for. But how was that possible? I couldn't return to Ynes Verleath now. I had to return to the courtly life. If Gillacoemgain was truly gone, so much would be in upheaval. Lulach and Crearwy were the heirs of Moray. I had an obligation to them. I would need to fight to protect what belonged to them.

I sighed deeply, not wanting to think of it. Lulach woke then. I picked the child up and rocked him. "Lulach for the world," I whispered as the tiny baby blinked, straining to look at me. "I guess we shall see."

❦

*M*adelaine came the next morning with breakfast. "Do you know what's going on?" she asked Sid and me, setting a tray on the table beside me. "Uald is frustrated. Epona is sullen. And there is a stranger here. No one will tell me anything."

"The stranger...she's a wet nurse," I answered.

"A wet nurse? For you? Did you ask for one?"

I shook my head.

"Then why did Epona bring her here?"

"To help her steal children," Sid answered absently as she stirred a cauldron hanging over the fire.

"What does she mean?" Madelaine asked me.

"Epona wants me to leave Crearwy here."

"What!" Madelaine exclaimed, waking Lulach who fussed at the interruption. "Oh, my little one," she said, lifting him, "I'm so sorry. Gruoch, I hope you told her no."

I looked at Crearwy who was still sleeping.

"I haven't decided."

"What in the world do you mean? You can't just leave her here."

"Imagine what your life would have been like if you had been raised here. Imagine if you had never been married off to Alister. If I leave Crearwy here, she will be free in a way neither you nor I ever were."

"But she carries royal blood."

Did she ever. "Which she will dedicate to the old gods, to the old ways," I said, making an argument I wasn't sure I even believed.

Sid turned and looked at me. "If you decide to do as

Epona asks, know that I will stay by her always, love her like my own. You have my word."

Madelaine eyed Sid warily.

"As would Uald," I told Madelaine, "and Epona, and all the others."

"Druanne holds no love for you."

Sid snorted. "She's all sound and fury. Her heart isn't as hard as she lets on, and she's a good teacher."

I raised an eyebrow at Sid.

"What? She isn't *all* bad," Sid said.

I shook my head.

A moment later, Epona opened the door.

Furious, Madelaine turned on her. "How could you?" my aunt demanded.

Epona took a deep breath and tried to stay calm.

"Madelaine, please," I said. "This is hard enough," I added then turned to Epona. "I don't like this. I don't want it. But I trust and love you. Bring the girl here. Let me meet her."

Epona nodded and left.

"You are stronger than me. I couldn't do this even if it is for the best," Madelaine said as she reached down to stroke Crearwy's cheek.

"Not Malcolm, nor Duncan, nor any other will ever rule her. As Moray's heir, her life would never be her own. Here, her heart is hers to give as she wishes."

"What about Lulach?"

"He'll stay with me."

Madelaine frowned. "Well, I'm sure Gillacoemgain will be pleased with a son, but you'll leave him to mourn his other child."

I said nothing. Until everything was certain, more than just visions, I didn't want to face what I suspected to be the truth. It was Gillacoemgain who was left to be mourned.

The door opened. Epona came in followed by a young woman with long, brown hair. She had a sweet face and bright green eyes. She smiled softly at me. Without being asked, she came and sat in the chair next to my bed.

"I am May, My Lady."

"Please, call me Cerridwen. I will start with an indelicate question. Have you a babe of your own or did you lose your child?"

May nodded, understanding, but sadness choked her. "My little one came early, was dead when I birthed him from me."

"Do you have any other children?"

"No."

"Your age?"

"Seventeen years."

"And the father?"

"The child was merry-begot. I did not know the father."

"Do you have any family who will search for you? Is

there anyone for whom, or any reason why, you would abandon my daughter?"

"No. None. I worked on a farm with some good people. I was an orphan. Uald used to come to us to trade and sell wares. She would talk to me, in a general way, about this place from time to time. Like you all, I was raised to worship the Great Mother. It fills my heart to be here. I would love to help raise your daughter amongst these good women and treat her as nicely as I would my own child. All these women will be your child's mother, and I can tell they all love you."

I studied her face closely. She was an honest girl. Her eyes held no deceptions.

"We should see if Crearwy will accept you," I said.

May nodded.

Epona picked up Crearwy and handed her to May.

I felt my heart break.

Madelaine looked away.

It took a little coaxing to wake the sleeping baby, but finally she was roused. Crearwy fussed at first, not wanting to take to May. With some coaxing, she latched on.

"Best let her feed a couple of days to make sure all will be well," Epona said.

"I despise everything about this," Madelaine told Epona.

"Elaine," Epona said softly, calling Madelaine by the Goddess name I'd heard used but once before, "this is for the best. Separate your wants from what is right for the girl."

"Easy for you to say. Crearwy will be with you, not with her mother, not with her kin," Madelaine retorted. "In the end, you get what you want."

I reached out and set my hand on Madelaine's shoulder.

Frustrated, she rose and went outside.

Sid lifted Lulach from the cradle and handed him to me. I pressed my cheek lightly against his head. His hair was as soft as silk. He let out a contented sigh.

"She's a pretty little thing," May said. "Like a little pixie."

Sid smiled.

"She's feisty though. Cries throughout the night," I told her.

May stroked Crearwy's cheek. "Lovely little lass. Crearwy…that's her name?"

I nodded.

"Sweet baby," May whispered. "I'll watch over her. You have my word."

I nodded but looked away, unable to control the terrible pain racking my heart to see my child with another.

Epona wrapped her arm around me and hugged me. "I'm sorry," she whispered in my ear. "I know…I know this must hurt, but please trust me. You're like a daughter to me. Please trust me."

"Us," Sid corrected.

"If anything goes wrong," I told Epona, "you must send her to me at once. You must not hesitate. If this place is…lost, you must return her to me. Sid must open the doorways and bring her to me."

"You have my word," Epona said.

I looked down at Lulach. "Let's be sure she takes to May. Then, I must go."

Sid set her hand on my shoulder.

I closed my eyes and prayed the terrible misery creeping across my heart would disappear.

Madelaine and I stayed amongst the women for two more days. May was able to keep Crearwy full and happy and cared for her despite Crearwy's angry protests. In the end, I liked the girl. She was intelligent, funny, and sensitive to my sacrifice. As much as I didn't want it, I knew it was time to return.

"Tomorrow, we must go back," I told Madelaine that evening as we sat by the fire. Madelaine held Crearwy, rocking her gently as May, who'd taken over Sid's cot, slept.

"We can stay a few more days. Uald met with Tavis this morning. He's doing fine."

I shook my head. "No. We must return."

Madelaine raised an eyebrow at me. "Is something...wrong?"

"Yes."

"Something...something bad?"

I nodded.

Madelaine sighed. "For one so young, you've had too much heartache. My heart is breaking. I cannot imagine how you must feel. I'll never forgive Epona."

"Promise me you'll see Crearwy as often as you can."

"Of course," Madelaine said, nodding.

A tear rolled down my cheek. I was trying to be strong, trying to do the right thing, but my heart hurt. After Duncan's violation, I never thought I'd be able to love my children. Now, I loved them more than anything. My heart felt so heavy.

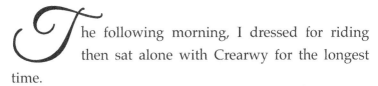

*T*he following morning, I dressed for riding then sat alone with Crearwy for the longest time.

"Don't forget me," I told the little baby.

I prayed that she would not begrudge me for what I had to do. The tiny baby looked at me with barely open eyes. My heart broke. I bade myself remember the Crone's words. But when I looked at her, all seemed lost. She was a part of me. How could I ever leave her behind? I panicked. I wanted the baby. I thought about

Lulach and how hard it would be for him without his sister. I thought of a million excuses to take Crearwy with me. But in the end, I knew what I had to do.

When I could take no more, I kissed the baby and opened the door.

Epona, Sid, and May came back inside. I handed Crearwy to Epona.

"I'll watch over her," Sid told me. "As will Nadia. We'll always watch over her. You have my word."

"Thank you, old friend," I said, squeezing her hand. It was then I made a promise to myself that when I returned to Cawdor, I would find Eochaid and keep him close to me.

Epona fixed her eyes on me. "This sacrifice is not in vain."

I nodded. "I know."

"Cerridwen," May said, embracing me. "I'll love her with my whole heart. I promise you."

I nodded then went outside. Madelaine and Uald were waiting.

In tears, I mounted Kelpie.

"Be safe. Be well," Uald told me.

"You too," I replied.

I looked back once more. Sid stood in the doorway of her house. Behind her, I saw May holding Crearwy, Epona hovering nearby. They were both smiling.

Sid raised her hand and waved farewell.

I turned and rode from the coven with Lulach hidden

under layers of clothes. Madelaine wept as I tried to freeze my heart. I couldn't allow myself to feel. I couldn't allow myself to process the loss of my child. So much uncertainty was headed my way, and I needed to be strong for Lulach.

It seemed like it took forever before we met Tavis.

"But one child lived," I heard Madelaine tell Tavis. It surprised me to know she would lie, even to him, to protect Crearwy. But she did.

"My boy," I told Tavis who kissed the sleeping babe on his forehead.

"Handsome little lad. I...I'm sorry about the other child. Do you think the journey from Moray..."

"No," I said, not wanting Tavis to take on any guilt for nothing more than a lie. "It was just not meant to be."

Tavis nodded. "All the same, I am so sorry. Let me get ready so we can leave at once," he told me, moving quickly to break down his camp. How loyal he'd always been to Madelaine and me. True love and loyalty were hard to come by. With Banquo, I'd had love. With Gilla-coemgain, the relationship had started as loyalty but had blossomed into more. I clutched Lulach tightly, squinted my eyes hard, and prayed my vision had been false. I prayed that Gillacoemgain was alive. I thought of how he would feel, how proud he would be, when he saw Lulach. The image filled my heart with endless joy...and sorrow.

We rode off, leaving the coven, and my daughter,

behind us. My heart ached. It was too much. I tried to close myself from my emotions as nagging pain started to creep across my head. My body, fresh from childbirth, hurt. I was exhausted. My heart broke for Crearwy, and there was an ache in my chest for Gillacoemgain. My hands started to shake. A sharp pain shot from temple to temple. Gritting my teeth, I forced myself to stop thinking, stop feeling, and ride ahead toward an uncertain future.

CHAPTER TWENTY-SIX

*I*t was dusk when we arrived at Madelaine's keep. The snow was falling lightly. The sky was bathed in a deep red color as the sun set. The castle was a black silhouette against the early evening skyline. I could see the glowing blobs of torchlight moving inside the castle. Outside, however, it was eerily silent. All the hairs on the back of my neck rose as we passed through the castle gate.

"See what the matter is," Madelaine whispered to Tavis as we dismounted.

Hurrying, Tavis headed into the castle. Wordlessly, one of the stable boys took the horses. A few moments later, Tavis and Ute came outside. Ute held a torch above her head. The flame made a patchwork of orange light and black shadows dance across her face, but I could see her eyes were red and puffy from crying.

"Oh, My Lady, thank goodness you have returned," she said.

"What has happened? Why is everyone so quiet?" Madelaine asked.

"My Lady," Ute said, turning to me as she fought back tears, "word has come that," she paused, cleared her throat, and then said, "that Gillacoemgain and fifty of his men were burned to death in a fire. Lord Macbeth and Lord Thorfinn have won the war. We've had word that Duncan is racing from the south and Macbeth from the north to lay claim to you."

Madelaine gasped.

My body shook.

It was true.

He was gone.

"Ute, dress in your riding clothes," I said.

"My Lady?"

"We ride north…for Macbeth."

ABOUT THE AUTHOR

New York Times and *USA Today* bestselling author Melanie Karsak is the author of *The Airship Racing Chronicles*, *The Harvesting Series*, *The Celtic Blood Series*, *Steampunk Red Riding Hood*, and *Steampunk Fairy Tales*. The author currently lives in Florida with her husband and two children.

KEEP IN TOUCH WITH THE AUTHOR ONLINE

facebook.com / melaniekarsak

twitter.com / melaniekarsak

instagram.com / karsakmelanie

bookbub.com / authors / melanie-karsak

pinterest.com / melaniekarsak

amazon.com / author / melaniekarsak

Alphas and Airships

Peppermint and Pentacles

Bitches and Brawlers

Howls and Hallows

Lycans and Legends

The Airship Racing Chronicles:

Chasing the Star Garden

Chasing the Green Fairy

Chasing Christmas Past

The Harvesting Series:

The Harvesting

Midway

The Shadow Aspect

Witch Wood

The Torn World

The Chancellor Fairy Tales:

The Glass Mermaid

The Cupcake Witch

The Fairy Godfather

Made in the USA
Coppell, TX
03 July 2021